PLAYED BY THE BISHOP

THE MURDOCH MAFIA SERIES
BOOK 1

SAMANTHA BARRETT

Cover by Leah Maree at Designs by LM.

MJ,

My mini me, my overachiever, but most importantly my son.
I love you beyond measure. This series is for you, my boy.
Reach for the stars, baby, and never let anyone hold you back.

Author Note

This book may make some uncomfortable with the content.

I have always sworn if I ever wrote mafia I would go dark in order to stay true to my characters, and that is what I have done. Some scenes and descriptions may make you uneasy, make you feel squeamish but rest assured there is a HEA.

For those who have read my PNR and thought they were dark, well this is worse, so much worse but in the best possible way.

Welcome to the Murdoch Mafia Family and all their fucked-up shit.

Chapter One

Kiara

Start before you're ready, don't prepare, just begin.

That is the motto I have been living my life by since I was eight years old. A shudder rolls through me at the thought of having to share a dorm with Carlina Murdoch. I'm going to have the hardest fucking time of my life being her room-mate. I don't know how the administration staff could have fucked up so bad as to room me, a scholarship kid, with the princess of the biggest mafia family in the country.

I stare at the dark wood door, reach out and grip the handle ready to push it open, then stop. What if she's in there? What do I even say to her? This whole school is crawling with rich entitled fuckers, each and every one of them looks like their mommy and daddy still wipe their asses with gold paper. I should be happy that the school let trash like me in. I busted my ass for this full ride and I will not let any of these fuckers take it away from me. I'll die before I ever go back to that hell hole I crawled out of!

I take a deep breath and turn the handle, shove the door open and walk in. My eyes widen and my brows jump up to my hairline when I see... *pink*. The whole fucking room is decked out in pink everything! The fucking walls are pink, the curtains are even pink and, fuck me sideways, both beds are decked out with pink bedding and fluffy pillows to match. This is my worst fucking nightmare!

I may be a girl but I'm not a fucking girly girl. I'm from the Bronx and the closest thing I had to something pink in my room was getting my period once a month. I trudge further into the room and claim the bed that is closest to the window. Each of us has our own desk and closet but there is only one bathroom. I drop my tiny-ass suitcase and duffle on the bed, then open the window. The room reeks of her perfume and it's making me nauseous.

I close my eyes and inhale a breath of fresh air. I can do this, I have to do this. I won't let the fact I am rooming with Carlina deter me and my goal. Having a school like Beckett Heights Academy on your college applications goes a long fucking way in getting you into the college you want. The sound of the door opening has me stepping back from the window and turning to face my roommate. We stand here sizing the other up. She's changed. Her hair isn't short, it cascades down to her waist in luscious waves. Her brown eyes still hold the innocence of a child. She has a diamond stud in her nose that I'm sure costs more than my dump of a house. The heels she wears don't do shit for her height, she's still short as fuck, but they suit her. Her pencil skirt and blush-colored blouse blend perfectly with her tanned skin. Carlina is the epitome of a mafia princess, even if she doesn't know it.

"Kiara?" she whispers my name like she's seeing a ghost. I guess for her it would seem that way. Her shock bleeds way to hurt and I start to feel like a bitch for ghosting her all these years. But, if she knew the truth, her eyes would no longer hold that innocent look.

"Hey, Car, it's been a minute." She places her hands on her narrow waist and cocks her hip to the side. A mask falls over her face and I know she is about to start ragging.

"It's been a minute?" Her imitation of my voice pisses me off. "That's what you have to fucking say to me after ghosting me for fucking years?" I fight the cringe that wants to roll through me. I can't tell her the truth. If I do, it will be my head on a spike.

"Look—" She holds her hand up silencing me and that shit grates on my fucking nerves.

"No, I don't want to hear your excuses, K. You fucking just up and left after everything!" Shame washes over me. Out of everyone in this world, I wish I could have turned to her but who the fuck would believe trailer trash like me?

I left Carlina to unpack or whatever the hell she was doing. I couldn't stand to look at her and for her to see the betrayal in my eyes. She was my best friend. She didn't care that I was poor or that I didn't wear designer clothes or that I was the maid's daughter. She just saw me. I walk around the campus aimlessly, not really seeing anything or taking in my surroundings. I know I need to pick up my lady balls and face Car if we are to spend the semester together or however long as roommates. We need to find a way to get along and put the past behind us. That is easier said than fucking done, though. What her father did shaped me into the person I am today. Tony Murdoch is the lowest piece of shit I have known in my life. He is a con artist and a snake!

Get your shit together, Kiara!

I berate myself as I make my way back to the dorm ready to try to resolve this conflict between C and I, but as soon as I enter the room I am greeted by girlish giggles and squeals of laughter. I pause in the entryway and balk at the sight. Carlina and six other girls are sprawled out over both our beds and one sits in my desk chair. At the sound of the door closing they all turn to face me. I glare at Carlina who just rolls her eyes.

"Ladies, meet my bore of a roommate, Kiara." One of the bitches with shit-colored hair laughs.

"She's named after *The Lion King*?" The others laugh along with her. I clench my hands into fists at my side and take a deep breath.

"Considering her brothers are all named after chess pieces, I wouldn't be mocking my name!" I snap at the snotty bitch. I'm used to people looking down their noses at me and my threadbare clothes but that doesn't mean I have to stand here and take it on the chin.

"Oh, please. You *think* because you read news on the internet that you actually know the Murdoch brothers?" One of the other girls snickers, the sound of her nasally voice grates on my nerves. To my surprise, Carlina actually speaks up instead of letting her posse continue to make assumptions.

"She actually does *know* my brothers." Their mouths drop open like those turning clown heads from the circus. Their gazes swing to me in shock.

"I know, right? How could someone like me know Bishop, King, Knight and Rook? The travesty of this situation, am I right?" Their shock bleeds way to outrage and I smirk at each of them. One of the girls hops off *my* bed, places her hands on her hips, flicks her red hair over her shoulder and runs her gaze over me.

"Is she the charity case your dad took in, Lina?" I scrunch my face up at the nickname. Car hated people calling her that when we were kids. I choose not to dwell on the fact she called me Tony's charity case, that man does nothing for anyone except himself. "Look at her, there is no way your brothers would even take a second look at someone as pathetic as her." I roll my eyes.

"Well, just for your FYI, darling, *they* know me very, *very* well. Just ask about me, boo boo." I don't stick around. I grab my towel and head into the bathroom, locking the door behind me and resting my head against it. I had planned to keep my nose clean and stay out of trouble whilst I finish out my last year of high school. Being able to board here was the best perk. It meant I got to get away from my mother and the city she used as her playground... the corners she would stand on for *work*. I may have fabricated the truth a wee bit. I know the twins Rook and Knight, they are younger so they were around Car and I more than the other two. King was around but he's older than us so he wasn't around as often as the twins. Bishop, well he is an enigma. A ghost in the shadows. You may not have seen him but you could feel his presence all around you. He's the oldest of the five of them and by far the most dangerous as he is next in line to take over his father's empire. Bishop was the star of many of my dreams. I've had a crush on him since the first moment I met him all those years ago.

I remember trying to catch his eye when I was younger,

something about him called to the darkness inside me. On the rare occasion he was around, a sense of safety would wash over me. Bishop makes you feel safe and cared for just by him being in the same room. I've read the tabloids, heard the stories and rumors that people make up about him. Gone is the boy who could make you feel like he would protect you from the monsters. He's been replaced and remodeled into the person his father wants him to be—a cold-blooded killer. I just need to survive this year and then I'm done. I can get as far away from my past as I can, where no one knows me or my mother. I just need to get the fuck away from New York and never look back. The farther I get from the Murdoch's, the better off I'll be.

Chapter Two

Kiara

I wake the next morning and smile to myself. This mattress felt like I was sleeping on a cloud. I turn onto my side and glower. My roommate may be a princess to the mafia but she sleeps like a fucking farmer. Her hair is wild and untamed, her mouth hangs open as small snores tumble out. I can see a small trail of dribble coming from the corner of her mouth and cringe. She may look like a man's wet dream during the day but first up in the morning, she looks like a dogs ass. I decide not to disturb her and steal the first shower, I refuse to be late to my first class. I may come from nothing but I'm *not* nothing. I've kept good grades my whole way through school and that won't change now just because I go to some swanky-ass private school on the other side of town. I shower and change whilst Carlina still sleeps. I shake my head and go about making my bed.

"How did it feel sleeping on 500 thread count sheets?" I finish setting up on the cushions on the bed before turning to face Car. She's sitting up stretching, taking her time. I check the clock on the wall and furrow my brow.

"You know you only have an hour before class starts?" Her face scrunches.

"Your point?" I grit my teeth in frustration, of course she wouldn't care.

"Don't worry about it." I snatch my schedule off my desk and grab the books I'll need for the day and shove them in my bag. I turn and head for the door but her question stops me.

"Why did you disappear?" I grip the strap of my bag tightly and count to three in my head trying to ward off the rising panic inside me. If I turn to face her, she will see the truth in my eyes. I keep my back to her as I answer.

"Why didn't you come find me?" Her shocked gasp is the last thing I hear before I walk out. The hallway is bustling with students, I have to slink against the wall so I'm not knocked over by two guys racing past me on electric scooters. I hide behind the curtain of my long black hair and keep my head down as I make my way to the cafeteria for a quick breakfast. I made sure to allow extra time in case I got lost trying to find my way to my first class today.

I push through the doors of the cafeteria and am assaulted by laughter and so many voices mingled together. I feel gazes on me but ignore them as I grab a tray and join the line. I pile my tray with eggs, toast and fruit. I snag a bottle of OJ and turn to face the crowd. There isn't an empty seat in sight. I decide not to loiter and head outside. I find a spot under a tree and take shelter under its shade. I rest back against the trunk and gaze around the quad as I eat. I smile to myself when I see a group of guys wearing letterman jackets, shoving each other and laughing boisterously amongst themselves. I envy how they appear carefree and like nothing in the world matters to them.

I spot a group of cheerleaders coming round the side of the building. They giggle and laugh at something the redhead bitch says, the same red head that is friends with Car. I honestly expected to see Carlina amongst them. She always loved cheer and she was actually good at it when we were kids. I almost kid myself into thinking I could try out for the same team as Car. What a fucking idiot I was back then to think someone like me would ever have a shot. I don't look like those stick figures. I have an *ass* and hips and my tits are a too big to fit into those crop tops. My long black hair would stand out amongst their blonde and light brown colored hair and my blue eyes tend to make people stare, they are so pale they almost look white. I'm also short as fuck and people always underestimate me because of my height. I may be small but a girl like me had to learn how to woman the fuck up and learn how to fight. Gage, he was my saving grace. He taught me how to fight at his gym. He took pity on me when he saw four guys corner me down the alley next to his gym, if I didn't have that piece of two-by-four I would have been raped and left for dead. He took me in and gave me somewhere safe to lay my head, somewhere my mother's *friends* couldn't try to come in and help themselves to my goodies.

"Holy fuck!" I shake my head and turn back to the pack of guys and find them staring at me. My eyes widen slightly when I register who two of the guys are. They break away from their group and head toward me. Not wanting to be in a weak position, I push to my feet and stand as both of their hulking forms dwarf my own. I look to each of them and no matter how hard I try to remain unaffected, I fail at keeping the smile off my face. Time may have carried on but their boyish charm still remains. "Come here!" His brown eyes shine with warmth as his brown hair flops forward onto his forehead. He shakes it away and wraps his arms around me. I don't even hesitate, I wrap my arms around his waist and inhale, he smells like home. He's so much taller than me that he practically hunches over my head.

"Fuck off, Rook, my turn." Rook and I pull apart. I turn to face Knight and smile wide. They are identical—exact same shade of eye color, hair color and even skin tone. I don't know how I do but I have always been able to tell the twins apart. I hug Knight and allow myself for just a second to think about how things might have been different if Tony hadn't done what he did. Maybe I wouldn't be so hardened inside and out and keep people at arm's length. But I guess that's what happens to people when their mother sells them to a fucking monster and doesn't care what he does to them as long as she gets her hit. We break apart and I gaze up at each of them. I may be older than them but there is no way these two would need a fake ID. they are huge and filled out. I know football players are big but these two are like over the top big. Their letterman jackets strain against their arms, they aren't even able to snap their jackets closed. I can feel their muscles and chests as they hug me—there isn't an ounce of fat on either of these boys. "You look good, princess." I roll my eyes at their stupid nickname. They have been calling me that since they watched *The Lion King* when they were younger.

"So do you—both of you look great." Rook and Knight exchange a look and I know they are doing that weird twin thing, where they can read each other's thoughts just from a single look. I tamper down my annoyance and wait. I can feel the eyes of their peers and the bitch squad on me but ignore them. I check the time on my phone and groan, my first class is due to start soon and I need to move my ass or risk being late. "I'll see you both around." Before I can step around them Knight shoots out an arm blocking my escape.

"What's the rush? We haven't seen you in years and already you want to escape us?" I flinch at the accusation in his tone. "Did... did we do something?" I deflate and look at both the guys and the vulnerability in their gazes has me crumbling. I reach out and grip each of their hands in mine, squeezing reassuringly.

"You guys didn't do anything." I can't tell them the truth but I'm also not a liar. I fucking hate being caught in a situation like this. "Things went to shit at home and I... moved out." It's not a lie, I'm just not telling them the full story of what really happened. Rook looks confused at my omission. Knight being the more intuitive one keeps staring at me waiting for me to say more. Before they can ask me more questions, two of their cheer squad slide in on either side of them linking their arms through theirs. I fight the eye roll that wants to break free. Each of the carbon copy Barbies run their gazes over me and scrunch their fake-ass noses in disgust.

"Are you the new janitor?" I narrow my eyes at the whore that clings to Knight. He glares down at her but doesn't untangle himself from the cunt either.

"No, you thirsty bitch. Now if you'll kindly get the fuck out of my way, I have a class to get to." I don't bother to wait for a reply as I push through Rook and Knight. I ignore their calls for me to come back. I hate to admit it but them not sticking up for me stings. Aside from myself, there is only one other person I can rely on to have my back, but he isn't here. I keep my head down as I make my way to my first class. I find it with ease thanks to actually paying attention when I was given a tour of the school. The door is open so I waltz in and claim one of the seats at the back. I gather the supplies I'll need from my pack and place them on the desk. I hear someone drop into the seat beside me and tense on reflex. I sit up slowly and peer over to see Knight staring straight at me. "What the hell are you doing in here?" I snap.

"I'm in this class," he says like it's obvious.

"You're a junior, this is a senior class. Don't fuck with me, Knight. I don't need any distractions." He narrows his eyes and pins me with a frosty glare that has me clamping my mouth closed.

"Since when did you give a shit about getting good grades?" I sigh and slump back in my chair. I decide to be honest and give him the whole truth.

"Since it was my only option to get a better life and not end up like my mom." I'm grateful when the bell sounds and other students filter in, effectively shutting down Knight's line of questioning. I barely concentrate through the class because I can feel his stare on me the whole time. I take notes and write down what I need to catch up on. As I look around and see other students with iPads and Laptops, I cringe. All I have is a pad and pen. I hate that I still feel inferior to others because of their money. I should be used to it. I knew this school was full of rich snotty bastards, but knowing about their wealth and seeing it are two totally different things. The bell sounds and I quickly shove all my books into my bag and race out the door before Knight can catch me. I know it's stupid but being around the twins and Car again is bringing up memories I fought fucking hard to repress. I will not go back down that black hole again. If it

12

wasn't for Gage, I don't think I would have made it. I wanted to die and was prepared to give up, without me even knowing it Gage became my reason to fight to live. He's my best friend. He never pushed me to talk or open up. He's always just been there for me for the past three years since I ran.

———

I don't even think as I fill my tray with food, then head straight outside to enjoy the sunshine. I'm not in the mood for all the stares and prying eyes. I just need to keep my head down and get the fuck through this year, then I'm free. I'll finally graduate and be able to get the fuck out of here and move to Alaska. I want to live out my dream of being isolated amongst nature and not having to deal with people day in and day out. I'm not anti-social, I just don't like people. They annoy the fuck out of me. I claim my spot from this morning and set my tray to the side as I pull my books out, prepared to get a start on the work I need to catch up on. Apparently, my public school isn't quite on par with this private school's curriculum. I shove a piece of pineapple into my mouth and pick my pen up when a shadow falls over me—wait, scratch that, *shadows*.

"Well, fancy running into you out here, again." I grind my teeth together as I slowly raise my gaze to meet the twins' stares. "Can't have you eating alone now can we, princess?" I open my mouth to protest but then Rook waves over his football buddies and I gape at the audacity of them.

"Are you fucking kidding me?" I grit out through clenched teeth. Knight meets my gaze and I can see the cunning monster that lurks beneath the surface of his care-free playboy façade.

"My brother has a point. What type of friends would we be if we let you eat on your own?" I glower at the shithead.

"We're not friends, Knight!" I hiss.

"Ouch, that actually hurt my feelings." I turn to Rook and scowl. "Come on, K. Don't be mad. You may actually like the guys, they're cool." Speak of the devils, their posse sits around in a circle casting us side long glances. I make sure to keep my resting bitch face in place as I run my gaze over each of them. Rook and Knight drop down on either side of me, so I take a deep breath and try to reign in my temper.

Suck it up, Kiara. They'll get bored of you soon and move on.

I keep repeating that mantra in my head as I eat my lunch and try to get a head start on my homework. When the bell sounds, I don't even utter a word to any of the guys as I stand and head to my next class. I feel eyes on me and look to my left as I climb the steps to the science building and cringe. The bitch squad all sit around a picnic table glaring at me. I spot Car amongst them. A pang of longing shoots through me and I quickly shut it down. She was my best friend. My only friend aside from the twins and because of her piece-of-shit father, I lost her.

Chapter Three

Kiara

Two weeks

They're still not bored of me, the twins sit with me every day for lunch with their posse. Okay, maybe they're not so bad. Knight has made sure to let his whole defensive line know I'm off limits and anyone who thinks I'm not, will answer to him and Rook. I gave them shit about that but truthfully, I don't give a shit. I don't have time for dating or fucking. Monday to Friday I work my ass off at school. Friday and Saturday nights, I'll be fighting at Gage's gym—making some good money, I might add. Rook has asked me where I disappear to over the weekends and I lie. I'll never tell him or Knight that I fight. Carlina and I coexist but that's it. We don't speak to each other in our room, which suits me just fine because I work better in silence. The course load here is fucking intense, it's kicking my ass daily but I've never been more... happy? I scoff to myself, what the fuck would I know about being happy. The bedroom door slams open and I peer over my shoulder to see Car walking in with her arms full of bags.

"No thanks, I'm fine." I stare at her in confusion as she glares at me.

"What?" Her upper lip pulls back in annoyance.

"Don't offer to help or anything!" I snort.

"You bought that shit, you carry it." I shake my head and turn back to focus on my English essay that needs to be finished by tomorrow.

"You're a real bitch, you know that?" My anger sparks. I clench my pen so hard I fear I may snap it. "You know what, happy fucking birthday, you bitch." Something smacks me in the back of the head. I push back from my desk and stand, shooting a glare at the pampered princess in front of me.

"Why the fuck did you do that?" She drops the rest of her bags to the floor and places her hands on her narrow waist as she stares at the ground near my feet. I follow her gaze and that's when I see a pair of all white Converse's laying on the floor next to my feet. I stare at them like they are a foreign object.

"Happy birthday, Kiara." Her whispered words shock me back to reality. I scoop them up from the floor and slowly lift my gaze to hers. Car may be able to fool every other girl here with her mask of indifference but I can see straight through it. The look in her eyes tells me she is nervous about how I am going to react to her buying me a... gift.

"You remembered," I say, barely above a whisper. She huffs and rolls her eyes.

"Of course I did. It's not a day I'm able to forget, no matter how hard I try." I nod unable to speak as a lump forms in my throat. No one has ever cared about me like Carlina. She would always share things with me as a child. My deadbeat, broke-ass, drug addict mother never fucking bought a single thing for me. I always wondered about who the hell my father was. I gave up trying to find him and was just grateful for the cheque I would get each month from him. The man is a loser but at least he is smart enough to put the cheque in my name and not Moms or it would end up being liquid gold in her veins, as she called it. "Are you going to say something?"

"T-thank you." She scoffs and grabs another bag from the ground then tosses it to me. I catch it with ease and stare at her for a beat before she motions for me to look inside. I slowly open it and will my emotions to stay in check as I peer inside the bag and smile. I pull a photo from the bag and run fingers over it, remembering the day this was taken. Tony was out of town and my mom was off somewhere, so I stayed with the Murdoch's. It's one of the only pictures of the six of us together. Car and I stand in the middle with a twin at each of our sides. King stands behind Car and Bishop stands behind me. I remember feeling so nervous and self-conscious with him being so close to me and wondering if his heart was beating as fast as mine, or were they in sync with each other? I remember the smell of his cologne and the heat of his body pressed against mine. The way his mere presence surrounded me and made me feel complete for the first time in my life.

"It was the last summer we spent together before you... took off." I hate the note of vulnerability I hear in her voice.

I lift my gaze to hers and the look in her eyes destroys a part of my soul. I hate Tony Murdoch more than I ever thought possible, he not only destroyed me but stole the only people in this world I ever cared for. "Why did you leave?" The watery tone of her voice hits me like a dagger to the heart. Would she believe me if I told her the truth? Car has always been a daddy's girl and I may have been her best friend, but who would take the word of their friend over the person who created and raised them? I place the items on the foot of my bed and take a deep breath trying to work up the courage to even broach the subject of my leaving.

"I never meant to hurt you, Car—"

"But you did! You broke my fucking heart, Kiara. My brothers and I searched for you and when the trail ran cold, Bishop went to dad to ask for his help. We fucking thought you had died until you show up here for orientation!" I stare at her in shock hearing that Bishop would do anything like that for me. Guilt eats away at me for the pain I caused them all.

"I never meant to worry any of you or make you feel abandoned, Car. You all were the family I never had and leaving you guys was and still is the hardest thing I have ever had to do in my life." She closes the space between us and grips both my hands in hers, her gaze bores into mine pleading with me to let her in on my darkest secret.

"Why did you have to leave though? We were all happy and I know you wouldn't have left because of your pathetic mother. She was fired three weeks after you disappeared. The bitch never said a word about your whereabouts no matter how many times we asked after you." My mother had no idea where the fuck I went. After I ran from the Murdoch's is when I met Gage. He gave me a roof over my head and a place to feel safe. If it wasn't for him, I honestly don't know if I would even be here right now.

"S-something happened and I just had to get away." Car isn't having any of my half-truths. She narrows her eyes and chews on her bottom lip. I know her so well and can tell she is trying not to push me too hard and risk me running again.

"Whatever happened, you can tell me. I just want to help, Kiara, I swear." I open my mouth ready to spill but decide against it. I yank my hands from her grasp and spin away, for one fucking moment I thought I might actually be able to tell her the truth but I was a fool. Of course she would think her father is a savior. "Don't shut me out!" I peer out the window and will my emotions to stay in check, I can't let her see me crumble.

"I don't want to keep you in the dark, Carlina. You're the one person I wish I could have run to and asked you and your brothers to protect me, but I couldn't." I hear the anguish in my own voice and it pisses me off that even the thought of him can reduce me to a pussy.

"Protect you from what?"

"The monster that parades around like a saint," I whisper, then slam my eyes closed and will my tears back.

"Who are you talking about?" I shake my head. No one, aside from Gage, knows the truth about what transpired.

"I'll always love you, Carlina, but I can't. You wouldn't believe me and honest to God, I don't blame you for that. I wouldn't believe me either." She grips my arms and spin me around to face her, her eyes are rimmed with tears.

"Kiara, I swear to you, I will believe whatever you tell me. Me and my brothers will never allow anyone to hurt you." The conviction in her tone has me wanting to crumble. I feel the unshed tears behind my eyes.

"What if I told you I ran because of your father, would

you believe me then?" Her eyes widen as she drops her hold on me and stumbles back a step. I shake my head as I see her begin to wall off her emotions from me. "I told you that you wouldn't believe me. Can we just forget about the past and move on?" She reaches up and covers her mouth with her hand, shaking her head from side to side. I stand tall and wait for her to lash out and accuse me of being a liar, that her father is a good man.

"He raped you too, didn't he?" She may have spoken the words quietly but I stumble away like she screamed them in my face. I grip the window ledge for balance as I peer at her in shock. My mind is reeling and I can't even think straight or form any words to answer her. Tears threaten to spill as reality comes crashing down around me. How the fuck does she know? She wraps her arms around herself as if trying to hold herself together, drops her chin to her chest and quiet sobs begin to wrack her tiny frame. I want to go to her and comfort her but I'm too stunned to even move. She said, *he raped you too*—what the fuck does that mean? I decide to block out all my warring emotions and comfort my friend— my best friend. I never stopped loving her or missing her. I never blamed any of them, except for Bishop. I wrap my arms around her and hold her tight as she breaks down in my arms.

I sit with my back against the headboard of Car's bed and her head in my lap as I stroke her hair. She finally stopped crying about twenty minutes ago but neither of us have uttered a single word, too lost in our own thoughts. I want to ask her so many things but I can't get my fucking mouth to open. I want to push for answers but seeing the way she broke and screamed like she lost one of her brothers keeps me from asking. Whatever Car endured at the hands of that man is clearly just as bad, if not worse, than what I went through.

"I was six when it started." I startle at the sound of her voice, but continue to stroke her hair and remain silent, giving her time to sort through her thoughts. "He would come in each night and give me a bath. It started with him washing my hair, then it moved on to him washing my body, then... he started to do other things. At first, I loved that he wanted alone time with just me. He would spend so much time with my brothers daily and I would be left out. What a fucking idiot I was, right?" She doesn't need me to answer that. "After a while I knew what he was doing wasn't right. A part of me thought it was normal for a father to touch his daughter this way. I mean, I didn't know any better I was fucking six!" A sob bursts from her and I hate Tony so fucking much more in this moment then I ever have before.

"You did nothing wrong, Car. You were a fucking child. He took advantage of you and he's a piece of shit!" I try to take some calming breaths and tamp down my rage. She needs me to be silent and listen to her vent, not hear me raging on about how much of a cunt her father is.

Chapter Four

Kiara

Four weeks

Car and I may be on common ground now but we still have an elephant between us. She opened up to me and when it came time for me to return the favor, I clammed up and couldn't even utter a single word. I know she feels betrayed by me, but it took me over a year and to be a bottle of Jack Daniels deep before I even told Gage.

"Yo, you there, K?" I shake my head to clear my thoughts and focus back on the conversation that the twins, Quinn and Garrett are having. I smile sheepishly and shrug my shoulders.

"I may have missed the question." Knight scowls at me

but I ignore him. He has been pushy as fuck lately. I don't know if Car disclosed what happened between us to her brothers. I will not be the one to discuss her private business, I would hate for that to happen me.

"What are you planning for the break?"

"Nothing much." I can see Rook isn't happy with my answer and I really don't give a shit. Since being here, Gage has cut me out of the fights and told me I need to focus on my schooling—easy for him to say though. No fights means no money, which equals me being fucking strapped for cash.

"You gonna be staying here?" I shake my head in answer to Quinn's question. He and Garrett are the only guys out of the team aside from the twins that I actually like. They're not like the others that continue to make passes at me daily. Ever since I punched the team's wide receiver for grabbing my ass, the team no longer sits with us under my tree.

"Why don't you come back with us?" Rook's question is innocent enough but it still causes me to stiffen. When I spy Knight out of the corner of my eye, I know he saw my reaction to his twin's question.

"You going back to your mom's?" Knight's question draws an involuntary scoff from me. My eyes widen, fuck!

"I mean, yeah I'll go home." I can feel Rook and Knight staring at me but refuse to meet their gaze, then stand before making a lame-ass excuse about needing to hand in a paper and quickly scurrying off.

───────

After grabbing dinner, I head to my room. I don't even think twice about Car not being here when I arrive. I decide to utilize the alone time to get some of my homework done and grab a shower. As I lay in bed and check the time on my phone, I begin to worry when I see it's after curfew. She may be a rebel but even Carlina Murdoch doesn't miss curfew. It's only a Tuesday, so I know there isn't any parties on tonight. Maybe she stayed in a friend's room? Even as the thought enters my mind, I know deep down inside myself that Car wouldn't do that. She is a stickler for sleeping in her own bed.

I lay awake for hours waiting for her to return. When I check the time again and see it's two in the morning my worry turns to unease. I may not like the cheer bitches but even I know they wouldn't be out this late with them having early practice in the morning. I haven't seen Car hang out with anyone else aside from them. I debate texting Rook or Knight but decide against it in case I am just blowing this shit out of proportion.

I startle awake at the feeling of having someone watching me. I bolt upright in bed and scan the room. I don't see anything at first until I spot Car's desk chair and see a shadow in it, staring directly at me. I freeze, I knew he would find me. How could I have been so stupid as to think being at the same school with his kids wouldn't lead me directly to me, he's come to finish the job.

"Just fucking do it!" I grit out through clenched teeth. I'm so proud of myself for sounding so strong and my voice not wavering to give away the fear I feel inside.

"Do what?"

Oh my God.

The sound of his voice washes over me like a warm caress. The deep baritone and the husky sound has goose-flesh sprouting all over my body. I slowly reach over and flick on my beside lamp, then slam my eyes closed so I can adjust to the light. I blink them open slowly and bite my lip as I run my gaze over him. His gaze bores into me with an intensity that has me wanting to squirm beneath the pressure of it. His large frame fills the chair. He leans forward and rests his forearms on the tops of his thighs, causing his suit jacket to tighten around his bulging biceps. I see tattoos on the tops of his hands. His suit fits him perfectly. He has the top few buttons on his crisp white shirt undone, his brown hair ruffled like he has been running his hand through it continuously. A five o'clock shadow covers his jaw, brown eyes holding an intensity like no other. I sit here staring at him for so long my mouth is dry from swallowing over and over again. My anger begins to rise the longer we sit here with no words spoken. A knock on the door causes me to jump. I glare at him when I see his lip lift in the tiniest smirk. The door opens and I wait for Tony to walk in and finally kill me but it isn't him.

"Hey, princess." My mouth drops open and my brows raise in surprise, he takes a step toward me and I scramble off the bed to meet him halfway. King wraps his arms around me and I cling to him. We break apart and I smile up at the black sheep of the family. King has similarities to his sister and brothers, but he is the fairest out of the five. The only one with tinges of blonde through his hair and he also has green eyes, unlike the others. His perfect white teeth are on display as he smiles down at me. King is just as tall as the twins. He rests his hands on my shoulders and the feeling of his hands on me snaps me back to reality. I pull back from his hold and his smile falters slightly at my retreat.

"Why are you here?" I ask as I keep my gaze solely on King and not his older brother who can suck the oxygen out of a room just by being in it. King steps back until he stands beside Bishop. I reluctantly pull my gaze from King as I look at Bishop. Just the sight of him has me weak in the knees. Why did the one man in the world that brought something to life inside me have to turn out to be a bastard?

"Where is Carlina?" The accusation and anger in his tone has me wanting to cower. I hold his stare as I answer. Bishop Murdoch will not come in here and try to intimidate me after everything I have endured.

"How the fuck would I know where your sister is? I'm not her fucking keeper, Bishop!" He pushes out of the chair so quick it topples over. He closes the space between us in a second. His hand clamps around my throat, then he shoves me back until I'm bent over the side of the bed with his huge frame looming over me. For one second... one split second, I'm transported back to the moments where I was helpless and unable to defend myself. I'm not her anymore, I'm stronger. I strike out and punch him across the jaw. His eyes widen in shock. I do it again but this time he's quicker and catches my fist with his free hand, then pins it to my side. I lash out with my other arm and clip the side of his face before he draws his face back. he tightens his hold on my throat until I'm gasping for air. I look to King out of the corner of my eye, pleading with him to help me. His brows are drawn in and I can see he is torn between helping me and being loyal to his brother.

"Where. Is. Carlina?" He makes sure to enunciate each word, like I'm simple. I claw at his hand around my throat and try to break free of his hold. He's too big, no matter how hard I fight I'll still lose because men will always be able to overpower us females and there isn't a fucking thing we can do about it. I stare up at Bishop and resign myself to the fact that I am going to die at the hands of the man that I thought gave a shit about me. Just as my vision begins to go fuzzy and I start to see black spots he releases his hold on me and steps back. I gasp and cough as I drag in lungfuls of air whilst grasping at my chest. "Grab her, she's coming with us." I want to protest but I can barely breathe, let alone get any words out, as King grabs and hoists me over his shoulder.

Chapter Five

Bishop

She sits nearly on top of the door handle to be as far away from me as possible. King meets my gaze in the rearview mirror. I know he doesn't agree with how I handled her or even bringing her with us but until I find my sister, she is my number one suspect. Rook peers back at her from the passenger seat and the apprehensive look he shoots her tells me he is with King on this one. He thinks she is innocent. Knight is the only one in agreeance with me and doing whatever needs to be done to get Car back. I swore I would always protect her and I fucking failed. I sent her to this school with the twins, knowing they would watch out for her daily, but somehow they still managed to fuck up the one job I gave them. I don't care if they feel like shit, once we get back to the manor they will feel the real wrath of my fury. They want me to treat them with more respect like I do King, yet they can't even do one simple fucking job!

"We making a stop?" I grind my teeth at King's question. I'll deal with that fucker later for touching what was never his to begin with. I gave her time to come around and live her life how she saw fit for a while but that didn't involve fucking the enemy.

"Not tonight, go straight back." King grunts and focuses back on the road. Rook peers back to Knight in the back seat, I know they are doing their whole twin silent communication thing and it grates on my nerves. "Got something to share?" Rook shakes his head and focuses back out the window. Knight being the uncaring bastard that he is speaks up.

"How did you find out?"

"You don't need to worry about that. You should be more focused on what I'm about to do to you both when we get back." Knight scoffs. I turn and stare directly at him so he can see the anger in my gaze.

"You can blame us all you want but none of this is our fault. You brought this upon all of us when you decided to go rogue. You're not our father, Bishop, and you don't call the fucking shots." If he wasn't being such an arrogant asshole I would be proud of him for finally standing up to me. Out of my three brothers, Knight has always been the one to challenge me and never just accept what I say. Before I get a chance to answer him, we pull up to the Manor. Kiara still doesn't move or even make a sound. This girl used to be a part of our family and spent more time here with us then she did at her own home, until she just stopped. I climb out and make my way around to her door. I scowl at King when I see him helping her out of the car and wrapping an arm around her waist to hold her up. I grind my teeth so hard at the sight that they begin to ache. He's my brother and I would die for each of them but seeing him with his hands on her, causes the monster inside me to rear its ugly head.

"What's that?" I look to where Rook is pointing, that's when I see a box sitting in front of the front door. I pull my gun from my waistband and shoot King a look. He motions for Rook to take over his hold on Kiara. Knight moves into her other side and King pulls his gun from the holster beneath his jacket. Kiara doesn't even bat an eye to the sight of our guns. I move in front with King just behind me as we climb the couple of steps that lead to the porch. A plain box sits there. King comes up beside me and we exchange a look. He crouches down to open the box as I wait with bated breath to see the contents. He opens the flaps of the box and pulls out a creamy colored scarf. He holds it out to me and I stare at it as I run it through my hands and pause at the end that has a splatter of blood on it. I know with everything inside me that the blood on this scarf belongs to Carlina.

"What is it?" I hand the scarf back to King and when he sees the blood his whole body tenses. "Who the fuck would have the balls to take her? No one even knows about Car. We made sure of that!" He's right, even when she was born, Tony made sure that no one knew she existed in case they tried to come for her. Car was nothing but a bartering chip for him. He had always planned to marry her off to one of the rival families and use her marriage as leverage for more power. The bastard always had an ulterior motive for everything that he did. Nothing Tony Murdoch did was ever self-less, everything he did was always for his own gain.

"I don't know. Go make some calls and figure out who the fuck knew about her. If you need to use force to get them to talk, do it." King nods and heads inside to do as I asked. He is loyal beyond measure and family means everything to King, so I know our sister being gone is hitting him fucking hard. I turn back to the twins and Kiara and see the twins both have a look of blood lust in their eyes. They may be the youngest of the family but the both of them have a thirst for blood that is unmatched by me or King. I make my way down to them and order them both to go in and help King with whatever he needs. Rook is reluctant to leave Kiara alone with me. It pisses me off when she gives him a small nod and he finally concedes. She doesn't get to fuck off for years and then come back and call the shots. I fucking call the shots around here. "You will help us find her." A whoosh of air escapes her and she slumps slightly from fatigue, dropping her gaze to the ground. I follow her sight and curse myself when I notice she isn't even wearing shoes and it's fucking cold out. I bend and grip her behind knees and lift her into my arms bridal style. She doesn't protest or even fight, just wraps her arms around my neck and rests her cheek against my shoulder as I carry her inside.

I climb the stairs to the second floor, passing Mav and Luka on my way to my room. Neither of them says a word about the girl draped in my arms, even though I can see the curious looks in their eyes. I carry on down the hall and walk straight through my doorway and kick the door shut behind us. I place her on her feet and grip her waist until I'm sure she is able to stand on her own. Unlike most girls she doesn't pull away and gawk around the room, just stands there and looks at me with those strange, pale-blue eyes that make you feel like they can see into your soul.

"I'll help however I can but I don't know where she

went, Bishop." The sound of my name from her lips has me yearning to hear her scream it as I fuck her raw.

"She didn't go anywhere... She was taken." She darts her tongue out to moisten her lips and I track the movement with my eyes, while standing before me in a plain white shirt that reads *Lannister in the streets, wildling in the sheets* and a pair of black boy shorts that show off her muscled thighs. I know she doesn't do any extracurricular activities, so what the fuck is she doing to stay in this good of shape?

"How do you know? She could just be staying with one of her friends or something." Even she has to know how dumb she sounds right now. Carlina doesn't do sleepovers, never has. I quirk a brow at her and she sighs. "Yeah okay, that isn't something she would do."

"Stay here, I got shit to do."

"Am I your family's prisoner?" Her eyes spit fire at me and I love the challenge I see in her gaze. I reach out and brush my knuckles against her cheek. I relish in the shudder that rolls through her from my touch.

"Not my family's, just mine. Now stay here, sleep, shower or whatever the fuck you want but you are not to leave this room until I say otherwise."

"No one knows who the fuck I am talking about," King roars as he slams his drink down beside him on the counter. The four of us with Luka and Mav have gathered in the kitchen. I have an office but it's never used when times like this arise. Tony would make us stand around his desk as children so we always knew he had the power. That is not how I want to reign as Don of my family. I want to be able to lead my family fairly, not rule them by fear but by respect. My men follow me and are loyal to me because I treat them right, unlike Tony who ruled everyone, even his own children, by beating them into submission.

"Does the princess know where she is?" I scowl at Rook, I hate that the three of them still call her that.

"Her name is Kiara." I feel Knight's gaze boring into the side of my head but choose to ignore him.

"Why are you so touchy about her?"

"Shut the fuck up, Rook. Find our sister and then you can all go back to your carefree lives." Knight moves to stand beside his twin. King, Rook and Knight all glare at me.

"We never fucking asked you to do what you did. You decided to do that on your own and we all stood by you." I refuse to allow them to see the guilt I feel for that decision and the repercussions it had on each of them. My spur of the moment decision cost not only me but my siblings as well.

"I did what I had to do in order to keep you all safe. Don't ever question me again, Knight." I can see the anger swirling in the depths of his eyes and know he wants to argue but won't dare risk my wrath in front of Mav and Luka. They may be my brothers, but I am still the head of this family and will do as I see fit. I don't ask permission for shit.

Chapter Six

Kiara

I move around his opulent room and marvel at the wealth of it. Gold trimmings line the wall of his black room. Everything in here has its place—it's all so straight and neat that even his fucking sheets and comforter are tucked in at the corners. I move to his bathroom and groan at the sight of his clawfoot tub and huge open shower with one of those fancy as fuck shower heads that sprout from the roof. His toiletries are even lined up perfectly on the vanity. I head toward his wardrobe and roll my eyes. Everything in here is color coordinated and not one shirt sticks out further than the other... even his slacks are hung up. Does the guy own a pair of fucking sweats? I spot a plain black jersey in the back and snag it off the hanger, I pull it over my head then sigh as the smell of him assaults my senses. It's so long it stops just above my knees. I decide to take it off and place it on the bed. If I'm going to be stuck here for a while, I may as well enjoy my time.

I walk out of the bathroom after taking the best shower of my life. I lift my arm and sniff my skin, I smell like him after using his body wash. I cringe at the thought of having to put the same panties back on, so I decide to go commando. I pull my boy shorts on and fold my shirt and panties and place them at the end of the bed. I tug his jersey over my head and love the warmth it gives me. My feet are cold so I go in search of some socks, find a pair in one of the drawers in the closet and pull them on. The fucker is that tall, the heel of his socks rest on the back of my calf. I run my hands through my hair and flinch as I snag a knot. If he was going to kidnap me he could have at least packed me a fucking bag. I see the sun beginning to rise and decide that sleep is just not going to happen.

Fuck it.

I open the door and when I don't see any of them in the hallway, I quietly creep toward the staircase in the hopes I can steal a drink and some food from the kitchen. I know my way around this house like the back of my hand and even though I hate this place, even I can appreciate how beautiful it is. The walls are cream and lined with gold trim around the top. The only places in this house that aren't painted cream are each of the rooms, that was the one thing Tony relented on. He allowed his children to pick the color of their rooms. I tiptoe down the stairs and round the corner past the living room. As I pass Tony's office in order to make it to the kitchen, fear grips me in its clutches, my breaths come in short rapid pants as memories assault me. That room holds nothing but darkness and pain for me.

"Find her, now!" The sound of Bishop's booming voice

has me nearly jumping out of my skin in fright. "I don't care what it takes. Find out who the fuck took her and bring her back." I take a deep breath and give myself a mental pep talk. I close my eyes and run past the closed door of Tony's office as goosebumps dot my skin. I burst through the entryway into the kitchen and come to a screeching halt when I spot all four Murdoch boys and the two goons crowded around the bench. Bishop's glare promises pain and it sends a shiver down my spine.

"Princess—" B cuts Rook off.

"I told you to stay put." I roll my eyes and place my hand on my hip as I cock it out to the side.

"And I got bored. Sue me, asshole. You want my help, fine, But I am not going to stay put like a toddler just because you think you can order it!" He closes the space between us. The anger in his eyes has me backing up a step. For every step I take backward he takes one forward until I'm pressed up against the refrigerator and he's pressed against my front. I have to crane my head all the way back just look up at him. I hate being so fucking short! My head barely comes up to his chest and, judging from the smirk on his face, he is loving the height difference between us. He reaches out and wraps his hand around my neck. I keep my arms at my sides and don't punch him this time as his grip is firm but not enough to cause me to gasp for air.

"You will do exactly as I fucking tell you."

"Who died and made you boss, asshole?" A cruel smile stretches across his face and I stiffen at the victorious look in his brown eyes.

"Tony." I reel back so fast I smack my head against the fridge. I search his gaze trying to detect if he's lying.

"W-what?" I hate that my voice waivers.

"You asked who died. Tony died and I made myself

boss!" My mind reels with this new information—Tony is dead. The star of all my nightmares is dead and he will never be able to hurt me again. I slump against the fridge, making Bishops drop his hold on my neck to grip my waist so I don't fall to my knees. His gaze searches mine to try to decipher why I would have this type of reaction to the news of his father's death, but he will never figure it out.

"Boss." Bishop pulls me against him and wraps his arms around me lulling me into a false sense of security as he answers one of the goons.

"Speak."

"Gage Matthews is at the gate." I tense at the mention of Gage. How the fuck does he know I'm here?

"Let him in." I try to pull out of Bishop's hold but his grip tightens around me. I struggle against him and try to pull back using all my weight. My anger soars at the fact I am unable to dislodge myself, he's too fucking strong. Yet again, I'm simply at his fucking mercy. When I stop struggling, he finally releases me and I stumble back and hit my lower back against the marble top of the counter. I shoot him a death glare, then open my mouth to cuss him out but he speaks first. "Your boyfriend will be here in a second. If I find out you or him had anything to do with my sister's disappearance, I'll slit his throat in front of you." My mouth hangs open in shock, I've never heard Bishop sound so cold and callous before in all the years I have known him. A loud knock sounds out and I spy the two goons out of the corner of my eye as they make their way toward the front door. Bishop's gaze remains fixated on me, like a moth to a flame. I can't look away even as they return and I feel Gage's eyes on me.

"Baby doll, what are you doing here?" Bishop's upper lip twitches and the anger in his eyes intensifies at the sound of my pet name from Gage. I slowly swivel around and face my friend, but tense when I feel Bishop pressed against my back. Gage darts his gaze from me to Bishop and I see the confusion in his green eyes. He huffs out a breath and runs a hand through his chin-length blond hair.

"Gage—" King cuts me off and I grit my teeth in frustration.

"Where is my sister?" Gage pulls his gaze from me to stare at King, his brows furrow in confusion and I can see already that he has no idea what the fuck King is talking about.

"I don't know." B grunts behind me and I know before he even speaks Gage just fucked up. No one is supposed to know about Carlina's existence, Gage only knows about her because I told him.

"See, your answer should have been *what sister*, not I don't know. So now, we're going to have hurt you until you start speaking some fucking truth." Gage's gaze darts to me and I see it in his eyes, he's about to shut off every emotion he has and go into fight mode. G is a sweetheart and protective as hell but don't let that fool you, if you fuck with him or fuck him over, he will be the star of your nightmares.

"Bring it on, Murdoch. I'll beat all your bitch asses." He isn't lying. Gage is undefeated in the underground fight club with a 44-0 and all by knockout. Bishop wraps an arm around my waist causing me to gasp. He reaches around with his other arm, grips my chin and tilts my head up to face him. I stare at him in shock, as he slowly lowers his face toward mine. I start to heat and my heart is nearly bursting out of my chest the closer his lips get to mine. His eyes shine with lust. I gulp and wait. I wait for him to finally close the inch of space between us and kiss me, bringing all my childhood fantasies to life. His lips ghost over mine before he turns at the last minute to stare at Gage.

"See, I could have it anytime I want it. I don't even have to try and she's ready to spread her legs for me." I blink a few times as his words register. Shame washes over me and I push away from him. He releases hold on me and smiles cruelly like he just won some competition.

"What the fuck was that?" I snap, looking around and find the twins looking anywhere but at me. King looks angry but his glare is pointed at his brother, not me. I slowly turn back to face Gage and cringe when I find him staring straight back at me. I move toward him, needing to explain what he just witnessed in private, I owe him that much. As I reach out to grip his hand Bishop's words have my hand pausing midair.

"Touch him and you'll regret it." I peer over my shoulder and make sure he can see the hatred in my eyes.

"Go fuck yourself, Bishop. You don't tell me what the fuck to do. I said I'll help find your sister but I never agreed to be compliant and listen to anything you say." Fire swirls in the depths of his eyes as he scowls at me. I smirk at him as I grip Gage's hand in mine and shove past his goons leading G out to the back patio. I ignore Bishop's outburst and continue to pull Gage after me. I drop down into one of the pool loungers and motion for Gage to do the same. I tuck my legs inside the jersey and wrap my arms around them as I stare at the man who helped me survive. Gage isn't like Bishop, he doesn't wear suits as a form of armor, he doesn't need them. He wears low-slung jeans, black Chuck Taylors —low-cut of course because apparently high tops are for pussy's according to Gage, and a plain black tee that fits him like a second skin. We sit here and stare at each other. Never before has there been such a divide between us. I

SAMANTHA BARRETT

feel betrayed by him for not telling me that he knew the Murdoch's. "Why didn't you tell me you knew them?" Gage blows out a breath and drops down into the seat in front of me. He spreads his legs and rests his forearms on his thighs as he stares at me.

"I couldn't tell you, doll. I wish I could have."

"You work for them, don't you?" I brace myself for the answer that I know is coming, trying to prepare myself for the sting of his betrayal.

"No." Relief washes through me, but it's short lived. "I work *with* them." I turn away unable to look at him any longer. I trusted Gage more than I have ever trusted anyone, his betrayal hurts more than anyone could ever know. "I'm sorry, doll. I wanted to tell you so many times—"

"Then why didn't you? You had so many chances over the years to be honest and you fucking didn't. Why?" He reaches out and grips my chin, turning me to face him. His thumb strokes my cheek lightly, his gaze softening the longer he stares at me and I'll admit I melt slightly. Gage has always been able to soften me toward him just from one look.

"Because you knowing my business dealings with them put you in danger. When you told me about them... I couldn't tell you the truth after that. I never wanted you to look at me the way you are, Bishop is a prick but..."

"But what?"

"Bishop and I have known each other a long-time, doll." A question that has been sitting in the back of my mind blurts out of me.

"He knew I was with you, didn't he?" Gage's gaze hardens, he opens his mouth but I can see in his eyes he is going to lie so I push on. "Don't you dare bullshit me. I deserve to know the truth."

"Yeah, doll. He knew from the moment I took you in that night those fuckers tried to rape you." I nod my head numbly.

"Did you report everything to him?" I can hear the snark in my own voice.

"I never broke your trust, Kiara. I would never."

"Did you tell him we were fucking as well?"

"The fuck did you just say?" Gage is on his feet and spinning around toward the house where Bishop is storming toward us, his fists are clenched at his side. The twins and King stand in the doorway with the two goons standing behind them. Gage raises his hands and begins to rebuke my claim but Bishop is blinded by his rage.

Chapter Seven

Bishop

I punch him. He stumbles back a step but quickly rights himself and raises his fists, ready to go a round with me. I shuck off my suit jacket and tear open my white button-down and chuck them off to the side. I bounce on the balls of my feet and wait for him to attack. He swings out with a left hook. I dodge to the right but the fucker is quick and hits me with a swift right hook to the ribs. I swing back at him with a left, right combo and manage to land a shot to the side of his jaw. I strike out again but he drops down and springs back up with an uppercut that has me groaning and stumbling back a step. Both of us are panting and ready to go again but Kiara jumps in between us. She has her back to me and faces Gage. He immediately drops his fists to his sides. His features soften as he stares down at her. Oh, fuck off.

"You have feelings for her?" I laugh but there is no humor to it. He cuts his gaze back to me and his green eyes shine with malice. Kiara spins around to face me, the tiny devil has her pale baby blues narrowed at me. She opens her mouth to speak but clamps it closed when Gage presses up against her back. When she doesn't tense or push him back I see red. I strike out and hit him with a right hook over her head, then go for another hit but I'm stunned when she hits me with a solid left hook to the jaw and then a right uppercut that has me stumbling back a step. Gage wraps an arm around her waist, then twirls putting her behind him to shield her from me.

"Your issue is with me, not her."

"Get the fuck out of the way, now." Gage stands tall and refuses to move from in front of her. I can't be bothered with this shit so I wave for my brothers, Mav and Luka to come forward. Gage darts his gaze around at the others and knows he is outnumbered. Kiara reaches out and grips his hand urging him to back down, but Gage is too proud to admit defeat even when he knows he is losing. I smirk at the prick and relish at how tense he becomes when the others draw near. Mav and Luka come forward to grab him but stop short when Gage is tackled into the pool by... Kiara. We all rush forward and stare at the pair of them as they break the surface. I grit my teeth and glare down at her when she laughs. Gage stares at her for a beat before he joins in on her laughter. Tired of this bullshit I pull my gun from my waistband and aim it at Gage, both their laughter cuts off. I ignore my brother's protests as I speak. "Get the fuck out of the pool now, Kiara or I put a bullet between his eyes." She darts her gaze between him and me before finally doing as she is told. She swims to the edge and Rook offers her a hand, which she accepts.

"Bishop, please don't hurt him." I keep my gun trained on him as I turn to her. she has her arms wrapped around herself, shivering from the cold. That's when I notice she is wearing my jersey.

"You don't call the shots around here. Now go back to my room, I'll deal with you soon." I see the anger inside her rise. She bites her bottom lip and peers down at Gage, the fucker smiles and nods encouragingly at her. She shoots me one last seething look before stomping back inside the house. "Get the fuck out of the pool, now." Gage swims to the edge and no one offers him a hand. As soon as he's out I hand my gun to Luka and punch Gage right in the fucking nose and relish in the sounds of pain that tumble from his lips.

"What the fuck, you dick!" He pinches the bridge of his nose as blood pours down his face.

"Did you fucking touch her?" Gage sighs and I know just from the resigned look on his face that he fucked her.

"Yes." King lets out a shocked hiss, Knight whistles between his teeth and Rook just laughs like a fucking idiot.

"You have three days to clear out your shit and get the fuck out of my city before I kill you." I feel my brothers stares boring into me but I ignore them as I focus on Gage. He holds my stare and I wait for him to agree and grovel at my feet.

"I won't leave her."

"What did you just say?" My voice is barely above a whisper.

"She needs me, Bish. There is more you don't know and if you would drop all the bullshit, she would tell you!"

"You fucked her!"

44

"I didn't know who she was to you!"

"So that makes it okay that you fucked my future wife?"

"Your what now?" We all look toward the back door where Kiara stands with a horrified look on her face.

Fuck!

"Princess, why don't you go take a shower–" She keeps her gaze fixed on me as she cuts my brother off.

"Shut up, Rook." Gage shakes his head and turns to face Kiara. She pulls her gaze from me to look at him. "You knew about this?"

"I didn't find out until... after." She nods her head and it doesn't take a fucking genius to figure what he means when he says *after*.

"Hmmm. So not only did you lie to me, you also betrayed me in every way known."

"Doll—"

"Fuck you, Gage! I trusted you. I fucking told you... everything and you betrayed my trust by running to the fucking bastards that did this to me!" I furrow my brow in confusion. What the fuck is she on about? I look to King, who seems just as perplexed as I am. Gage takes a step toward her but she holds up a hand halting his movements.

"I never betrayed your trust, doll. I would never share what you disclosed to me."

"You're just as bad as him." Gage flinches at the cold harsh tone of her voice and drops his gaze to the ground. She shoots me one last scathing look before turning and storming inside the house.

"What the fuck was that?" Knight hisses, his gaze focused on Gage who is still staring at the ground.

"Dude, princess looked fucking pissed." Gage turns to the side and glowers at Rook.

"You have no fucking idea what you're talking about."

He storms off toward the house. I follow after him knowing he is going after Kiara and I'm not letting him anywhere near her alone ever again. King blocks my path and I snarl in his face. He stands tall and won't fucking budge.

"Say what it is that you need to say, then get the fuck out of my way!" I grind out.

"Something more is going on with those two. Figure out what it is so you can get your head in the game. Carlina is the priority here, not Kiara." I stare him down until he moves.

Chapter Eight

Kiara

I pull the wet jersey off and chuck it into the corner of the room, not giving a shit that it's probably ruining the carpet in Bishop's room. I grip the waistband of my boy shorts but freeze when the door bangs open. I use my arms to shield my chest, Gage's eyes widen.

"What the hell?" I yell. He shakes his head, his mouth dropping open in shock. "Turn the fuck around, now!" Gage nods like an idiot and does as I say. I dart into the bathroom but stop mid step at the sound of Bishop's angry voice.

"Get the fuck out now!" Gage nods and slides past Bishop who slams the door in his face. I glare at the asshole before stepping into the bathroom and slamming the door behind me. I grab a towel just as the door bursts open.

Bishop grips my arms and spins me around to face him. I drop the towel as I struggle in his hold to try and cover myself up.

"Let me go!" He gets right in my face. I make sure he can see the anger and hatred in my eyes.

"You like fucking that low life cunt?" I fight the flinch that wants to break free at his cold harsh tone.

"Let. Me. Go," I grit out through clenched teeth. He runs his gaze down my body in a possessive as fuck way that has the stupid part of my brain all giddy that Bishop Murdoch is looking at me this way.

"Did you like it?"

"What?"

"Did you like fucking him?" I reel back and narrow my eyes at the audacity of him to ask me such a question.

"Don't you dare look down your nose at me. Just because you have more money than fucking God doesn't mean you get to judge me. You don't own me, Bishop!" He laughs but it's a bitter sound.

"Wrong, I do fucking own you and the only reason that son of a bitch doesn't have a fucking bullet in his head right now, for touching what is mine, is because I need him for one more job. Oh, just so we are crystal fucking clear, the moment he touched you, is the moment he signed his own death warrant." He releases me and I stumble back a step whilst still covering myself with my arms.

"He didn't do anything wrong."

"He fucking touched you!" His angry shout has me recoiling slightly. I hate that Bishop is able to bring me to a scared mess. I've fought for years every Friday night at the shack run by Gage and some of those women were huge. I never flinched even as they landed blow after blow but all

Bishop has to do is raise his voice and I want to cower in the corner like a baby.

"He touched me, not you!" He cocks a brow at me and his eyes darken. I swallow loudly at the cold look in his gaze.

"By touching you he touched me. You're mine, Kiara, and the quicker you learn that the easier things will be for you." I shake my head, denying his claim.

"I'm not an object to be owned, B, I'm a person." He closes the space between us and reaches up to brush his knuckles over my cheek. My traitorous fucking body leans into his touch.

"No, baby, you're a fucking prize." His words have butterflies taking flight inside me. "And I won you years ago." The butterflies die inside me as my anger returns to take precedence.

"Fuck you," I snarl. He smirks as he drops his arm back to his side.

"Not today, baby. Got a lot of work to do. Shower and meet me downstairs in my office." I open my mouth to argue but he narrows his eyes and pushes on. "Defy me or keep me waiting too long, I'll put a fucking bullet through his kneecaps." I grind my teeth and nod my head. He smiles and opens his mouth to speak but I decide to get the upper hand here. I drop my arms to my sides, his eyes widen as they drop to my tits, I grip my waistband and push my shorts down. I can feel the heat of his gaze all over my body. I kick my shorts toward him and then face him with a brow cocked. I nibble on my lip and fight the smirk that wants to break free when his eyes track my every move. I'm actually quite stunned at how a girl like me can have someone like Bishop Murdoch entranced by just my body. I never thought this would be possible. I mean, I dreamed about it as a child but never thought it would actually happen!

Before he can even utter a word, I brush past him, step into the shower and turn the water on, hot. I feel victorious after rendering him speechless. I've never felt so powerful. My gleefulness is short lived when I feel the heat of his body at my back. I spin around so fast, I nearly fall down until he snakes his arms out and grips my waist to steady me. Our eyes lock and there is electrical current surging between us, the air around us begins to feel like it's crackling. I drop my gaze from his and stare at his chest, marveling at the intricate art work that covers every inch of his chest and arms. I want to reach out and trace the lines of his ink but fear keeps me rooted to the spot.

I prayed many a night that Bishop would come and rescue me from the horrors that would transpire inside the walls of this house, but he never came. I wished nightly that he would turn out to be my knight in shining armor, but he isn't anyone's knight. I pull back from him and shake my head willing the tears to remain hidden. I have worked too fucking long to allow him to see me break. His gaze searches mine and suddenly I feel so vulnerable standing here naked in front of my childhood crush. He reaches out and cups my cheek. I respect the hell out of him keeping his eyes on mine and not allowing them to stray lower.

"Why am I really here, Bishop? Don't lie to me and say it's because of Car. Your family could find her without my help." His hand slides from my cheek to the back of my neck. Gripping me tightly, he yanks me forward until we are skin to skin. The feeling of him bare and pressed against me has my pussy fluttering to life.

"You're here because I ordered it. You will remain here until I say otherwise."

"Screw you. You think you know me because I spent years of my life here... well newsflash, asshole, you don't.

You barely spoke two words to me growing up and now you want to get all in my face and act like I owe *you* something. Boy, please." His grip on the back of my neck tightens and I grit my teeth to try to tamper the pain. He bends down until our noses are touching.

"I haven't been a boy in a long time. You'll do as I fucking say or I'll take out your punishment on that bitch, Gage." I scowl and try to pull out of his hold but it does nothing to deter him. If I was less of a woman, I'd knee him in the dick but even I know that's a bitch-ass move.

"I'm not marrying you, Bishop. I want nothing to do with this family and your father." For the briefest of moments his mask falters and I see regret in his brown eyes as they bore into me before he quickly masks it.

"Tony is dead. I put a fucking bullet between his eyes and took over the empire he loved so much. You will honor this marriage. If you think there is an escape for you, you're wrong. You will be a Murdoch." He releases his hold on me with a slight push. I stumble back and hiss when my back collides with the cold tiles. I glare at his back. My gaze, as if it has a mind of its own, travels down to his ass and fuck me, what an ass. I shake my head to clear those thoughts from my mind.

After drying off, I wrap the towel around myself and walk back into the bedroom. I see a pile of clothes on the bed and smirk. I guess he doesn't want me walking around in his clothes. That thought dies the moment I grab the pile and realize they are *his* clothes. A pair of black sweats that are going to be huge on me, a plain gray shirt and another black sweater. I don't want to fight, I just want to figure out what the fuck is going on here, find Car, then get my ass back to school so I can get the fuck out of this place. Now that I know Tony is dead, I won't have to worry about him finding me at school. I might actually be able to even enjoy my last year. I'm eighteen now. I can do whatever the fuck I want and that involves finishing school, getting enough money for a plane ticket and going to Alaska. I change into the clothes the heavy-handed bastard left out for me, then go into his closet to steal another pair of socks. I've had to roll the sweats at the waist at least half a dozen times.

I've never been self-conscious of my height before, but being around all four Murdoch brothers makes me feel tiny and weak and I will not have that. I clench my hands into fists and vow that I will not let them push me around or allow my childhood memories of them to cloud my judgment anymore. I walk down the stairs and stop at the bottom. As I peek to the left and see Rook and Knight chilling on one of the lounge chairs in the living room, I decide to go and see them. I mean if me stopping to chat with his brothers pisses Bishop off a wee bit, my petty ass will take that as a win. At the sound of my approach, they both look away from the TV. Rook smiles invitingly, Knight eyes me skeptically and it pisses me the fuck off.

"Princess, I must say that is definitely not an outfit I would have chosen for you myself." I roll my eyes and smile as I drop down beside him. He wraps his arm around my shoulders and pulls me into his side.

"Didn't really get a choice in what I wear." Knight snickers, I look to him and watch as he huffs out a breath in annoyance before standing and storming out of the living room. I look up to Rook who has a sad look on his face. "Rook?" He slowly lowers his eyes to me, I can see the pain in his eyes and it hurts my heart to see that look. I reach up and cup his cheek trying to smile comfortingly.

"Unless you want Bishop to beat my little brother, don't touch him like that." I drop my hand and pull back from Rook to stare over the back of the couch. King stands there with a disapproving scowl on his face. Shame washes over me, does he think I was just hitting on Rook?

"Fuck off, queen, the princess was just about to profess her undying love for me." I gape at Rook and begin to shake my head but he shushes me with a finger to my lips.

"Don't push him, Rook. He is dancing on the edge of his sanity right now. You fucking around with Kiara is going push him right the fuck over that line and this time, I don't think any of us will be able to bring him back." What the fuck happened to Bishop? "Princess, maybe you shouldn't keep him waiting, huh?" I remain silent as I nod. I shoot Rook a smile before letting King lead me to Bishop. I freeze just outside the doorway to Tony's office—well, Bishop's office now. I close my eyes and will my heart to steady itself.

He isn't in there, Kiara. He can't touch you again!

"Doll?" I open my eyes to see Gage and King both standing in the doorway eyeing me, their looking at me like I'm a ticking time bomb. "You good?" I nod and follow after them. King steps inside the office but Gage darts his arm out stopping me. I peer up at him. We stand here silently just staring at each other. We don't need words to be able to communicate, much like the twins. Gage and I know each other so well we can tell just from the others body language what they are thinking and feeling. Right now, he can tell I'm not okay and faking it till I make it. He knows the horrors that transpired in this fucking room, a shudder rolls through me at the thought. "I'm right here. Say the word and I'll get you the fuck out of here."

"Do that and it won't be just Bishop coming after you." I turn back to the hallway to see Knight standing there with a look of warning in his eyes. I don't know what has happened to Knight but he isn't the carefree, happy, loving kid he once was. Whatever happened must have been horrible for him to change this much.

Chapter Nine

Bishop

I lean back in my chair and glare at the fucker blocking her. She looks at him like he is able to solve her problems. Knight speaks and brings her attention to him. Gage keeps his gaze focused on her. The way he looks at her, like he has every right to stare at what belongs to me, has my trigger finger itchy to shoot the bastard in the fucking face. Gage may be an asset to my business but if he tries to fuck with what is mine again, I have no qualms about putting him six feet under. She turns back to Gage and pats his chest, indicating for him to let her pass. He drops his arm back to his side as she slides past him, her expression changing from curiosity to annoyance when she spots me glaring at her from behind my desk. King moves to the side and leans against the wall with his arms crossed over his chest. Knight shoulder checks Gage on way past to claim one of the chesterfields in front of my desk. I flick my gaze to the chair beside Knight. She sighs and shakes her head as she moves forward to drop down into the seat in front of me. Gage rests his hands on the top of the chair she occupies, the fucker meets my gaze daring me to do something.

I smile wide and watch as Kiara tenses, she knows shit is about to go down. King stands tall waiting for my next move. I move at lighting speed, jumping to my feet with a gun pointed directly at Gage's head. Kiara squeals in surprise.

"You gonna do it this time?" I flick the safety off and ready myself to pull the trigger but she jumps to her feet and stands on the chair, blocking my shot.

I growl out my annoyance. "Get the fuck out of the way!"

"You want to shoot him, you're gonna have to shoot me first." I can hear the slight tremble in her voice, the unsure look in her eyes tells me she is questioning her stupid move but won't back down. Gage grips her waist and lifts her from the seat placing her on the ground. She tries to dart in front of him but he nods to King to come and subdue her. "Touch me and I'll break your fucking nose, King." My brother cuts me a look. I give him a subtle nod. He reaches for her but she ducks and swings around landing a left hook to his ribs. He steps back. Her size gives her the advantage as she ducks again from his reach and lands a swift hit to his nose. It wasn't hard enough to break it but it sure as shit made him pause. He curses. Gage reaches out for her and she doesn't shy away from his touch when he grips her waist again. He opens his mouth to speak but no words come out when she jabs him straight in the mouth! I cut a glance to

Knight to find his brows are nearly in his hairline as he watches Kiara fuck up our brother and Gage.

"What the fuck?" Gage snarls at her as he cups his mouth with one of his hands as blood trickles out from between his fingers and a sense of pride swells inside me knowing my girl did that.

"Don't you ever pass me off like I'm chattel. Next time, I'll break your fucking teeth, got it?" Gage is seething with anger which puts a smile on my face. I lower my gun and clear my throat to garner their attention.

"Come here." I wait for her to fight me or tell me to go fuck myself but she looks to Gage, then back to me before sighing and making her way around the desk to stand in front of me. Gage's fists are clenched at his sides, King is silently ragging in the corner. If she was a guy, King would have shot her and never batted an eyelid. I run my gaze over her tiny form and fight the smirk that wants to break free, she looks better in my clothes than I do. I drop into my seat and turn toward her. She eyes me suspiciously when I flick my gaze to my knee. Her mouth drops open and she shakes her head. I place my gun on the top of the desk and that snaps her into action. She settles herself on my lap, tense and stiff as fuck. I wrap an arm around her waist as I turn us back to face the others. She keeps her head down, not wanting to meet any of the other's gazes. Good, she needs to learn that I'm the fucking boss and I call the shots, not her! "Sit the fuck down now, Gage. Knight, get Rook, Mav and Luka." Knight nods and leaves to do as I ask. Gage keeps his glare on me as he drops into the chair she just vacated.

"Can I sit over there?"

"You'll stay right where you are. Until you learn to do as you are told, this is where you will sit." She stiffens further and I don't miss the subtle shake of his head as Gage implores her to do as she is told. Knight comes back in with the other three trailing behind him. Rook's eyes widen when he sees Kiara sitting on my lap, Mav and Luka don't even bat an eye at her, that is why they are here. These two have proven time and again that they can be trusted and are loyal to me and my brothers. "I want an update on Carlina, Have any of the families made contact?" Mav steps forward.

"No. I've reached out to them all and none of them were even aware you had a sister. They have each offered up their men to help search for her."

"If they don't have her, then who does?" Rook's question is the one we are all thinking. Sure, I have plenty of enemies but not in my city. I spent months if not years building relationships with the Dons of the other families to smooth over the shit Tony had caused. We haven't had a single issue with any of them, until now.

"Have you checked the cameras at the school?" I ask Luka.

"Yes, sir."

"What about the ones in her room?" Kiara stiffens and snaps her head back to stare down at me, the fire and rebellion that shines in her eyes has the beast inside me wanting to push her further.

"You have cameras in *my* fucking dorm room?" she hisses. She is vibrating with rage and I can see her fists are clenched on her lap. I lean back and stare at her for a beat, making her stew in my silence. The longer it takes me to answer, the more she shakes from her rage.

"You didn't think you roomed with my sister by mistake, did you?" Her eyes widen a fraction when it sinks in. she knows I am the one who made her rooming arrangements.

"You knew?" I raise a brow at her before nodding. "How?" I reach out and brush my knuckles over her cheek and relish in the involuntary shudder that courses through her.

"Baby, do you really think you got a scholarship?" She jerks back so fast she nearly falls from my lap; I reach out and grip her waist holding her steading on my lap. Her eyes fill with betrayal. She looks over her shoulder at Gage.

"Did you know?" He shakes his head.

"I had no fucking idea, I swear, doll." The truth of his words settles something inside her. She turns back to me and walls off her emotions behind her mask.

"I would like to pull out of school. Whatever it cost you for me to go there, I'll pay you back." Her statement has me grinding my teeth and my anger soaring to new fucking heights.

"You won't be dropping out and you will not be paying a fucking cent!"

"I'm not your charity case, Bishop. I don't want your fucking money. Why can't you understand that? I don't want to marry you and become your trophy wife—"

"You don't get a say in the fucking matter. When you return to school, Mav and Luka will accompany you. I gave you your freedom. You're the one who found their way back to me, now I won't let you go again." She shoves me back but I won't lessen my hold, she narrows her eyes and slaps me. I hear the guy's hiss. I slowly turn back to face her. Whatever she sees in my eyes has her stilling. I can see she is shocked she hit me but that won't lessen her punishment. "Get out." The others don't fuck around. King grips Gage by his shirt and drags him from the room. As soon as the door clicks shut, I stand. She scrambles to wrap herself around me so she doesn't fall on her ass. I march across the room and don't stop until she smacks against the wall. She grunts but doesn't cry out or even attempt to wiggle free.

Her legs tighten around my waist and her arms remain wrapped around my neck.

"What are you doing?" The unease in her tone has me filling with glee. I reach up, grip her hair in my hand and yank it—hard. She hisses but doesn't scream out for help or try to break my hold.

"Whatever the fuck I want with you." She holds my gaze as she speaks.

"But why would you want to? How come you care all of a sudden what happens to me? I get the twins wanting to help or whatever, but you and King were never around when we were kids." I smirk darkly at her. She has no fucking idea.

"I was always around, Kiara. You just didn't know it unless I wanted you to know I was there. Don't act coy, you knew I was always watching you."

"You sound like a perv, you know that?" I shrug as I run my nose along the column of her neck and inhale her intoxicating scent.

"At first, I was just intrigued by you and your happiness. I never knew what that was like, nothing in my life made me smile the way you did daily. Then as the years went by and you grew, my fascination for you did as well. Intrigue turned to want, want turned to lust and now, look where we are because you caught the monster's attention." Her brow furrows as she gazes at me.

"You're not a monster, Bishop." Her quietly spoken words stun me. Out of everything I just said, that is all she heard? "I don't understand what is happening. Why now? Why after all this time are you doing this?"

"I had planned to wait until after you graduated, let you have your senior year of high school before I came and

60

claimed you but that changed." Her eyes search mine trying to detect if I'm lying.

"How did it change?"

"Carlina went missing. I was supposed to check out the school and search her room but then I saw you. I was only going to watch for a while and then leave." Realization crosses her features.

"I woke up and changed your plan." I nod. She runs her tongue over her bottom lip and like an addict, I follow her every movement. "I can't stay here, Bishop." Her softly spoken words have me breaking out of my trance.

"Until Carlina is back safe, you won't be going back to school." I see the fight return to her eyes so I decide to compromise. "The best I can offer is for you to collect all your schoolwork and do it from here. That is my final offer." She tries to fight the smile that wants to break free but fails.

"That wasn't so hard, was it?" I glare at her which causes a beautiful laugh to tumble from her lips. She really has no idea who she is or how fucking special of a prize she is. Kiara Coleman has no fucking idea she is really a Bennett. She has lived in squalor her whole life and still managed to stay off the street corners, never put a needle to her skin like her mother. I release my hold on her hair and cup both her cheeks between my hands. Her laughter dies immediately. We stare at each other for a beat before I slowly lower my lips toward hers. When there is a sliver of space between us, I pause, giving her a chance to back out. "If you fucking turn away and tease me again, I'll break your dick off." Just hearing that word come from her mouth has my cock hardening behind my slacks. I chuckle and pull back, electing a groan of frustration from her. I smile wickedly at her before smashing my lips against hers. Her shocked gasp allows me entry and I groan at the taste of her. I swipe my tongue across hers, pulling a long moan from her. She runs her fingers through my hair and grips the strands.

"I didn't expect that." I pull back from her and turn to find Rook, Knight and King all standing in the doorway with a pissed off Gage behind them glaring daggers at me. "Carry on, brother. We'll come back after you guys are... finished." I glare at Rook. Kiara cups my cheek and pulls me back to face her, smiles shyly, then nibbles on the corner of her lip before speaking.

"Can you put me down?" I roll my eyes and do as she asks, keeping my back to the fuckers in the doorway as I adjust myself. The sound of her girlish giggle has me peering down at her and narrowing my eyes. She rolls her lips over her teeth. I turn back to face my brothers and Gage.

"What is it?" King holds my gaze as he fishes a phone from his pocket and holds it up to me.

"Hey, that's mine!" Kiara attempts to go and retrieve it but I wrap an arm around her waist and haul her back against my front. She doesn't fight me, it fills me with pride when she softens in my hold and leans further into me.

"She got a message." The ominous tone of King's voice tells me it isn't just a message from a kid at school.

"You went through my fucking phone?" King spares her a look that has her clamping her mouth closed. King moves toward us and hands me the phone. I grab it and input the passcode. "Are you kidding me?" I stare down at her impatiently, she moves out of my hold and places her hands on her hips and glares up at me.

"What?" I snap.

"You know my fucking passcode?"

"I know your code to everything. I know your social

security number, what classes you take, your grades and where you sit daily." She spins away from me and looks to the twins. Rook smiles sheepishly while Knight just pins her with a bored stare.

"You little snitches!" she screeches and stomps her feet as she moves toward the twins. They move out of her way so she can leave. I smile triumphantly that I'm able to get under her skin. My smile vanishes when she grips Gage's hand and pulls him after her.

"You follow her and I'll burn your fucking house down." Gage pauses, he looks from Kiara to me and I make sure he can see in my eyes that I'm not making idle threats.

"He burns your house down, we'll burn his to the fucking ground. He wants to invade my privacy so now he can deal with my anger." She turns to me and I stand tall waiting for her to speak. "Did you have cameras put into Gage's house?" I see him tense beside her, grit my teeth and shake my head. "Thank fuck. Wouldn't want you seeing what went on there." I take one step forward and she high-tails it out of the room dragging Gage after her. Rook breaks out into fits of laughter. King slaps him on the back of the head earning himself a smack from Knight for touching his twin. I scrub a hand down my face and the curse beneath my breath.

"She is going to knock you down so many fucking pegs, brother." I snarl at my youngest brother. Rook is the only one who would speak to me that way.

"Fuck off," I mutter as I scroll through her messages and pull up the most recent one.

Unknown number – meet me and you will get her back.

I type out a reply.

> Me – where and when?

The reply comes almost instantly.

> Unknown number – The correct answer would have been who is this?

> Me – who is this?

> Unknown number – too late now, Bishop.

I growl.

> Me – who the fuck is this?

> Unknown number – A trade for a trade, give me Kiara and I'll give you your sister.

> Me – how do I know she is even alive?

I wait for a reply but it doesn't come. I hand King the phone so he can read over the texts. I pull my own phone out and dial Luka, he's our tech wiz and can crack any code known to man, he isn't one of the FBI's most wanted for nothing. He answers on the second ring.

"Yeah, boss?"

"Where are you?"

"Trailing the girl and Gage." My hold on my phone tightens as my anger soars.

"Bring her back here. I need you."

"Boss?"

"What?" I snap.

"She won't come willingly."

"Carry her if you have to. Get the fuck here now!"

Chapter Ten

Kiara

I don't even have a fucking chance to have a conversation with Gage before I'm swung over one of fucking Bishop's goon squads' shoulder and am being hauled back to him like a lost fucking dog! As soon as he places me on my feet, I strike to hit him but he jumps back. The fucker was prepared for me to hit him. I smirk triumphantly at the bastard. At least these assholes know I won't go down without a fight.

"Kiara." The sound of my name coming from him has me pausing. I decide to throw caution to the fucking wind and demand answers. I turn around and face the high and mighty king as he sits behind his desk. I spy the twins and King leaning against the wall to my left, the two goons are standing like statues to my right. Gage stands beside me and I know it's pissing Bishop off him being so close to me.

"Don't fucking, *Kiara*, me. You demand I listen to you but what for? You think because you pin me against the wall and get me wet that I'll suddenly bow down and not fight you?" I ignore the laughter coming from my left and push on. "You want me to be compliant and not be a bitch? Start telling me the fucking truth, Bishop. A guy like you doesn't just decide he has the hots for his sister's best friend after years. You're not the type of guy to want marriage either so why the fuck am I here?" He stands slowly and fixes his suit jacket before running a hand through his hair, slicking it back. I watch as a mask falls into place. Gone is the Bishop that I know and now standing in his place is the Don of the Murdoch family, leader of the five mafia families. His brown eyes hold no warmth, they are cold and empty as he gazes at me.

"You're here because you were promised to me years ago. Did you really think your mother was a maid?" I open my mouth to rebuke his claim but he carries on. "Your mother was a whore and a drug addict. The only decent thing she did was fuck your father and have you." I flinch at the coldness in his tone, Gage reaches out to place his hand on my back but stops when Bishop pins him with a look. "Touch her again and she won't be able to save you. I've let you live because of what you did for her but don't fucking mistake my kindness for weakness." Gage nods and steps away from me. "You want the truth?" I mull over his question for a second but answer,

"Yes."

"You are going to marry me because our marriage will bring the end to a war between two of the greatest mafia families. You are not a Coleman... your last name is

Bennett. You are the only heir to the Bennett mafia family. Your mother was brought here so Tony could raise you in his image and keep your father from attacking my family. Your father is the Don of the Bennett mafia in Florida." I can hear everything he is saying but none of it is registering with me. My mother was the maid here. She got hooked on drugs and sold her body to fund her addiction. Gage ignores Bishop's warning and wraps an arm around me, pulling me into his side. I suddenly feel cold. "I believe your father has taken my sister and wishes to trade you for her."

"How do you know that?" I slam my eyes closed and push away from Gage. I stare up at him as he slowly lowers his gaze to mine. I see it, right there in his eyes.

"You knew about all of this, didn't you?" Gage doesn't perceive to misunderstand my question.

"Yes, I found out not long after you started living with me." I nod, too numb to even form words. I trusted him more than I have ever trusted anyone in my whole life.

"Is that why you trained me?" I whisper.

"God, no." He reaches out and places both his hands on my shoulders, then bends down so we are eye level. "I trained you to fight so you would be able to defend yourself. I never wanted you to be in the position you were in the first night we met."

"What position?" Bishop asks. I can't even stand to look at him. Gage doesn't take his eyes off me as he answers.

"She was nearly raped. I stopped it."

"So you thought teaching her how to fight was the answer? You should have fucking brought her here to me!" I flinch at the sound of his booming voice. All the years I spent training to fight and harden myself against feeling any emotions and not even twenty-four hours of being near the Murdoch brothers, has all my training fleeing me.

67

"This isn't about you, Bish. Other shit happened and she needed me, not you." I close my eyes willing the tears of betrayal to stay put and not leak out. I knew Bishop had lied to me. It's the MO of this family, but what I didn't expect was for Gage to be in on all of this.

"I would like to go now... please." The only sounds that can be heard in the room is everyone breathing. I can feel all their gazes on me but I can't look at any of them.

"Doll——" I shake my head, cutting Gage off.

"I want to go now."

"Let me explain."

"I don't want to hear any of it," I whisper, wrap my arms around my middle and sniff. Gage reels back like I hit him. He can see the unshed tears in my eyes. I have only cried in front of Gage twice—the night he found me and the night I told him about Tony. I finally turn to face Bishop. He has an unreadable expression on his face as he eyes me warily. "I'll do the trade for Car, just let me know when. I'm going to walk out of this room right now and no one is going to follow me." He opens his mouth but I raise my hand halting him. "I won't run, I just need to be alone right now." I don't wait for an answer, I turn and walk out as quick as I can so they won't hear the first sob tear out of me. I race up the stairs taking them two at a time, run to the end of the hall and slam the door behind me. I rest against it and drop down as I finally break. I cry for the life that was robbed from me, for the father I never knew, for the pain I suffered because Tony Murdoch used me as a fucking pawn in a war I didn't even know existed. I cry for the best friend that I trusted, I cry for the boy I have wanted my whole life—who turned-out to be a monster just like his father.

I slowly blink my eyes open and realize I must have fallen asleep. I sit up and notice I'm in bed and not on the floor. I pat myself down and I'm grateful that I'm still in my clothes. I look to the side and see it's dark out. I must have slept the day away. Movement from the corner of the room catches my attention. The only light in the room is from the moon but even in the darkness I would be able to tell that it's Bishop that is sitting in the corner. I tuck my hair behind my ears and cross my legs under me as I wait for him to speak. My eyes feel puffy and swollen from crying earlier but I just don't have it in me to give a fuck what I look like. Everyone has lied to me and used me in some type of way. My heart is shattered. I'm woman enough to admit I have been in love with Bishop since the first time I saw him when I was six, he was twelve and I knew there was no way a boy like him would ever look at a girl like me. Now that I finally have his attention, I don't want it because he doesn't want me for me. He wants me so he can gain more power because of who my father is.

"Gage didn't betray you." His softly spoken words startle me from my thoughts.

"Yeah, he did and so did all of you." I hate how weak and defeated I sound.

"I never betrayed you, Kiara—"

"You lied to me Bishop, you knew who the fuck I was my whole life and didn't say shit!"

"I didn't find out until I was sixteen who the fuck you really were, Kiara. Tony told me then I was to marry you to unite the Bennett and Murdoch families. You were only like eleven or twelve at the time and there was no fucking way that I was agreeing to marry a child. Did I notice you? Yeah. Did I like you in that way? Fuck no. It wasn't until you ran from us when you were fifteen that I started to pay attention to the way you looked. When you turned sixteen and I saw you out with Gage, I paid closer attention. But, when you turned seventeen is when I really noticed how beautiful you are. Now that you are finally eighteen, I don't have to feel disgusted at the thought of finding you attractive, or wanting to fuck you. Mark my words, Kiara, you are mine and I am going to fuck you wherever and whenever the fuck I want." I balk at his crass words. I can hear the truth in each of his words and it shocks me to know he rebelled against the idea of this marriage as I know that would have pissed Tony off.

"You were never going to let me finish school and go to Alaska, were you?" He leans forward and runs a hand through his hair. He doesn't even have to utter a word, I already know the answer before he speaks.

"No."

"Hmmm."

"What does that mean?"

"I'm just not surprised, of course you would know what I had planned."

"I stayed out of your life as much as I could. Gage was just supposed to keep you safe and away from Tony." I tense at the mention of his father.

"What about Tony?" I hate that I hear the tremble in my own voice. He's fucking dead and yet he is still able to inspire fear within me. Bishop lifts his eyes to mine and everything inside me stills, as all the walls I built up around myself come crumbling down. My breaths come out in short rapid pants. I begin to shake my head denying what I already know but it's no use.

"He'll never touch you again, Kiara. I made sure of that." The conviction in his voice should comfort me but it doesn't.

"Y-you knew?" Disgust swirls inside me at the thought of Bishop knowing my darkest and most depraved secret. He stands and makes his way over to me. He sits on the edge of the bed facing me but keeps enough space between us to allow me room to breathe. That's the thing though, whenever he's near I can't breathe, I can't even think straight. If I was Superman, Bishop would be my kryptonite. He makes me weak and I don't know if I like that or not. He sees through my hardened shell and won't allow me to hide behind my bad attitude.

"I only found out not long ago. We searched for you when you ran. I didn't know you were with Gage until a couple months after you started staying with him. He reached out to me in an effort to get you protection. He didn't know at the time that we were the ones that you needed protecting from." I can't stop the stray tear that leaks from my eye. He reaches out and swipes it away. "I'm so sorry I wasn't there, Kiara. I was too wrapped up in my own shit to even pay attention to what was going on just down the fucking hall from me. That cunt was hurting you and my sister and I couldn't even protect you both." I launch myself at him and climb on his lap as I wrap around him. When his shock finally melts away, he wraps his arms around me and holds me close as I sob against him. I never knew how much I needed to hear him say those things to me. I wished he would save me from his father but I know now that was an unrealistic expectation I put on him. He was just a kid as well when it all started. He runs his fingers through my hair as I cling to him. I honestly didn't think I would be able to cry anymore after the amount I cried already today.

"I'm not broken," I mutter against his chest. He grips my hair and pulls until I have no choice but to pull back until he can see my face. His eyes dart all over my face before finally settling and the anger that swirls in his eyes stuns me.

"I never fucking said you were. Even if you were broken, Kiara, I would find every piece of you and put you back together until you were able to see that broken things are beautiful."

"Even after what you know, you think I'm beautiful?"

"You've always been beautiful to me, Kiara. It just took you longer than I thought to realize that yourself." I nod my head.

"Bishop?"

"Yeah?"

"I'll do what you want, I'll marry you, but..." I feel him tense beneath me. I know I need to tell him what I want now or I risk being swept up in this life of luxury and lose myself in him. I'm not that type of girl. "I want to finish school. I also want to travel and I still want to fight on Friday nights." A murderous look overtakes his features and it's me who is now tense.

"What fucking fights?" I furrow my brow confused for a moment before a broad smile stretches across my face. His eyes narrow and I laugh.

"You have no idea that I fight every Friday night at the shack?" I screech in surprise when he stands suddenly. I lock my legs around his waist and tighten my hold around his neck. He grips my ass and holds me in place as he walks toward the door and throws it open before storming down the hallway. "Where are we going?" His only response is a growl which earns him another chuckle from me, we descend the stairs and he squeezes the globes of my ass until I yelp in pain.

"Not funny now?" I glare down at him.

"You could at least put me down, I can walk." He scoffs before continuing to walk us through the living room and kitchen.

"And risk you jumping in front of him to stop a bullet? I'll pass." I freeze in his hold, fucking hell, he's going after Gage. I try to squirm out of his hold but he wraps his arms around me and keeps me in place. "Keep wriggling like that, baby. All you're doing is making my cock hard." I still and that's when I feel it, his cock bulging against me. My cheeks redden and I bite my lip, feeling shy all of a sudden. I'm not exactly experienced with guys. I don't count Tony as an experience. To me, Gage was my first sexual partner. The thought of knowing that I'm the reason Bishop is hard sends a thrill through my body and has my pussy clenching on air. I feel myself getting wet at the thought of him ploughing into me and making me come harder than I ever have before. "Thinking about my cock, baby?" I shake my head to clear my thoughts and that's when I notice he has stopped moving and we stand in the rumpus room. I look around and see the twins and Gage by the pool table with Bish's other man, Mav I think his name is.

"You been playing mommy and daddy upstairs?" I glare at Rook as he hides his smile behind his can of Pepsi.

"Actually, no. I was giving Bishop an *oral* exam." I smile sweetly as he chokes on his drink. Knight smacks his back which just broadens my smile. Bishop leans forward and kisses my cheek which stuns me but I don't let it show, I want to see how this is going to play out between B and Gage. I feel victorious that I actually did something he didn't know about.

"Fucking hell, doll, didn't need that mental picture." I open my mouth to sass Gage back but Bishop beats me to it.

"How about we fight it out at the shack on Friday night

after Kiara's match?" Gage visibly pales. He swings his gaze to me before focusing back on Bishop, I don't see what the big fucking deal is here. "You fucking let her into that ring?" I recoil at B's shout, he is legit vibrating with rage right now and it scares the shit out of me.

"She never fought under her own name, I made sure she was hidden."

"That wasn't your fucking call to make! I warned you what would happen, you chose to defy my order. Mav, take him." I struggle in Bishop's hold and try to break free as Mav leads Gage from the room, I call out to G but he ignores me and keeps his head down. I thrash in Bishop's grip but his hold is too strong.

"Put me down now!"

"Shut up. Kiara. You'll stay exactly where the fuck you are."

"Bishop!"

"I said shut the fuck up, Kiara!" I recoil at his harsh tone. How the fuck does he go from being sweet and tentative to a raging asshole in a matter of minutes? "Knight, shut down the fucking shack. Rook, get her shit from school and some clothes from her dorm." He doesn't wait for a reply, he exits the room and instead of heading back to his bedroom like I expect he turns left and goes out the back toward the pool house. For some reason I feel like I can breathe easier just by not being inside that house. He kicks the door open and storms inside. This place has had a makeover since the last time I saw it. The walls are painted white and of course adorned with gold trim. I scream out in surprise as he tosses me through the air and I land on the huge couch. Before I can sit up he pounces on me, his legs either side of mine, gripping my arms and pinning them above my head. I thrash about beneath him and curse him out but his grip still doesn't falter.

"Get the fuck off me, now!" I feel the panic inside me creep to the surface. I fight back the nightmares that taunt me and remind of a time I wasn't able to fight against someone and was at their mercy.

"I told you that I would punish you." I gape up at him and shake my head as tears threaten to spill. Whatever he sees in my gaze has his body going slack and his grip on my hands loosening so that I can pull free if I so wish. "I would never hurt you, baby. I'm not him." I sniffle and hate myself for it, I don't want him to think I'm weak. It's just been a fucking long ass day and I need to sleep, wake up again and hope this nightmare is over. "Your punishment is sleeping with me." I open my mouth to protest but he pushes on, effectively silencing me. "Not sex, just in the same bed as me. I brought you out here because I thought you would feel more comfortable in here rather than inside the house." I deflate a little at his carefulness.

"Okay." He releases my hands and climbs off me, then reaches out and offers me his hand. I eye it for a second before placing my hand in his. Once I'm on my feet and standing before him I expect him to lead me to the bedroom. What I don't expect is him kissing me. I stand here unmoving for a moment before it hits me that Bishop Murdoch is actually kissing me and I'm not dreaming. I open for him and moan at the taste of him. His taste overwhelms my senses and his presence consumes me. He grips my hips and I shiver at the feeling of having his hands and mouth on me at the same time, I grip the front of his shirt and pull it loose from his pants. I run my hands underneath his shirt and moan at the feeling of his skin, he groans as I run my fingers along his abs and up to his chest. I want to see and can't be bothered undoing all the fucking buttons, so I break our kiss, grip his shirt and tear it open. Buttons fly in each direction but I don't give a fuck,

"Well, that's the second shirt that got ruined today." I smirk but don't answer, I'm too enthralled by the artwork that covers his body. Bishop is fucking sexy in a suit and don't get me wrong, thinking about him in a plain pair of grey sweats and shirtless with all his tattoos on display has me clenching my thighs together to try to alleviate the ache between them. I trace my finger over the ink and smile. Skulls, knuckle dusters, guns, roses and so many other things cover his chest. I push his shirt off his shoulders and marvel at the ink that coats his arms and hands. "Like what you see?" I look up at him and smile.

"They're gorgeous."

"Wait till you see them on top of you." I can tell he's teasing me so I decide to play along, batting my lashes up at him and say,

"Want to show me?" I expect my response to catch him off guard or at the least cause him discomfort but no, he pushes me back until I fall on the couch and he jumps on top of me. This time I don't freak out. He runs his hand under my shirt and I shiver at the feeling of his hand being on my skin, continuing to shiver as he traces his fingers higher. He pauses and snaps his gaze to me when he reaches the underside of my breast.

"You're fucking killing me here, babe." I nibble on my bottom lip.

"I had no clean... undergarments?" I don't know why it sounded like a question instead of an answer but I'm embarrassed to tell him I'm naked beneath his clothes. He throws his head back and groans.

"Are you wearing any panties?" I roll my lips over my

teeth. When he looks at me again, I shake my head. "My cock is so fucking hard right now, it's painful." Feeling embolden by his statement, I spread my legs wider and allow him to slump forward. My eyes shoot wide open when I feel his hard cock pressed against my pussy. He smirks smugly and quirks a brow at me. "Baby, don't fucking tease me because I'll take what I want. You get a free pass tonight but rest assured, I'm going to fucking destroy this pussy very, *very* soon." He captures my lips in a heated kiss effectively silencing me. He grinds his pelvis into me and I moan into his mouth, the friction from the sweats and pressure from his cock thrusting against my wet cunt has me moaning shamelessly. My body takes on a mind of its own and I thrust my hips up grinding against his cock. A hiss escapes him and I reach up and grip the back of his neck holding him in place as I continue to taste him. He grinds against me and I moan so fucking loud he pulls back and smirks down at me. The cocky bastard knows exactly what he is doing to me and is loving every minute of it. "I want to taste you." It's not a question.

He doesn't wait for me to answer as he leans back, grips the waistband of my sweats and begins to peel them from me. He chucks them over his head, then drops his gaze to my pussy. He reaches out and grips my thighs, pushing them further apart. He whistles at the sight of my exposed cunt. I know he'll be able to see how wet I am for him. He uses his thumbs to part my folds—I'm not ashamed or even embarrassed that Bishop is staring at my pussy. I've known him most of my life and trust him not to hurt me. He shuffles off the couch gripping my legs, then yanking me down. I rest up on my elbows and take in the sight of him on his knees, the Don of the most notorious crime family is on his knees—for me. He grabs my legs and places each of them on his shoulders, uses his fingers to part my lips, then darts his tongue across my clit. I buck up against him as a moan tears from me. He hums his approval and buries his face between my legs. As he eats my cunt out, I slump back against the couch and lift my shirt so I can tweak my nipples. The sensations coursing through my body has me writhing beneath him.

"You taste so fucking good."

"Then stop talking and keep tasting." He chuckles but obeys me, pushing his tongue inside my entrance and holy fucking shit, I see stars. He fucks me with his tongue and I push against it needing him deeper. He pulls out and swipes his tongue up my slit then sucks my clit into his mouth. "Fuck yes, just like that." He keeps sucking and lapping at my clit until I feel like I'm about to burst. "Bishop!" I cry out.

"Come all over my fucking face." His crude words are my undoing. He sucks my clit again and I shatter beneath him, screaming his name so loud I'm sure the others can hear me from inside the house.

Chapter Eleven

Bishop

I push her legs off my shoulders and stand, pop the button on my slacks and push them and my boxers down in one swift move before stepping out of them. Her eyes widen at the sight of my cock, her tongue darts out to moisten her lips. I grip my cock, pump it twice, her eyes tracking my movements.

"Sit up and suck it." Her gaze shoots to mine. I quirk a brow daring her to deny me. The hazy look in her eyes tells me she will do anything in this moment if I make her come again. She shuffles forward and reaches out tentatively gripping my cock. I hiss as she pumps me once. "Wrap your fucking mouth around it and suck me down your fucking throat, now!" Like an addict, she does exactly as she is told so she can get her next hit. Her wet mouth is like fucking heaven, I throw my head back and groan. She sucks cock like a fucking pro, the perfect amount of suction and no teeth. She massages my balls in one hand while she uses the other to pump me whilst she sucks. I grip the back of her head and hold her there while I thrust as far as I can inside her mouth until she is choking, only then do I pull back slightly and let her breathe. She moves her hands to grip my ass and pulls me closer—my dirty girl likes choking on my cock. I look down at her and when I find her pale blue eyes staring up at me, I nearly cum on the spot. Most women wouldn't dare make eye contact while they suck cock. Not my girl though, she wants me to see her as she brings me to my fucking knees. I release her and pull my cock out of her mouth. She gasps for air. I grip her chin and use my thumb to smear the spit from her chin all over her lips before pushing my thumb inside her wet heat. "Suck."

"Hmmm," she moans around my digit and for the first time in my life I'm fucking jealous of a goddam finger! I yank it free and grip her shirt, yanking it off her. Her perfect perky tits peek at me, begging me to have a taste. I push her back and lean over her as I cup both her tits in my hands, kneading them. She moans and it spurs me on. I suck one into my mouth and flick my tongue across her taut bud. She squirms beneath me and tries to thrust her hips but I'm not about to rush this. I want to take my time and explore every inch of her fucking body. I switch to the other side and love the sound of the mewl that comes from her, I pinch her other nipple between my fingers and she gasps, "Bishop." I release her nipple with a wet pop, I use my knee to spread her legs open as I climb on the couch. Just the sight of her bare pussy has my balls tightening wanting.

"I'm not gonna be gentle, I'm gonna fuck you so hard you see stars but, if you're a good girl I'll fuck you again later and try to be gentle." She meets my gaze and I love the challenge I see in her eyes.

"Fuck me as hard as you want, just make me come." I love that she isn't shy to express what she wants. I grip my cock and swipe it up and down her pussy loving the moans that tumble from her lips. I don't warn her as I slam inside her wet fucking heat. She screams out and I flop forward bracing myself on my elbows either side of her head. She wraps her arms around my neck and yanks me down to her so she can kiss me. Her legs lock around my waist and pull me in deeper. I moan into her mouth. Her cunt is so fucking tight it's sucking the life out of my cock. I thrust inside her. She breaks the kiss moaning my name. I sit back and wrap my hand around her throat as I pull out, then slam back inside her. I do that a couple times before finally burying myself deep inside her pussy and fucking her like a rabid dog. The couch is too fucking soft so I grip her under her arms and lift her, while still keeping my cock buried inside her.

She doesn't say a word, just bends down and kisses me. I had planned to move to the bedroom but now, I'm just going to fuck her against the wall. I'm not gentle when I slam her against the wall, her pussy clenches around my cock and I smile against her lips.

"You like it when I fucking throw you around, don't you, baby?" Her only reply is to moan as she bounces herself up and down on my cock. Her tits are right in my face, so I grab one and bite down on her nipple, making her cry out.

"Fuck, Bishop. Just like that. I'm gonna come!" I release her tit and grab both her legs, then place each of them on my shoulders. Fuck, at this angle I can feel her G-spot. I slam into her and she screams out. I keep the same rough pace for a moment before she screams out my name as she comes all over my fucking cock. I fuck her pussy harder as I feel my impending release coming.

"You're gonna take every fucking drop of my cum inside this cunt!" Her eyes are glazed over from her release.

"Fuck, yes. I want you inside me, so fucking deep inside me, Bishop!" Fuck, her words spear the beast inside me. I slam into her cunt three more times before I roar out my release. I come so fucking hard inside her that I nearly see stars, her pussy clenches my cock milking it of all its cum. I take a second to catch my breath before I push her legs off my shoulders, pull out of her and grip her waist until I'm sure she is steady. She stares up at me in question.

"Clean the cum off my cock." Her eyes blaze with heat, I expected her to tell me to go fuck myself but she doesn't. She lowers herself to her knees and locks her hands behind her back and speaks,

"Fuck my face hard until your cock is clean." *Jesus Christ!* She opens her mouth and I thrust my cock inside. She wraps her lips around it and moans at the taste. I reach out and brace my arm on the wall as she sucks me clean. I can feel myself getting hard again already. I hope she had a good fucking nap today because I'm going to be buried balls fucking deep inside her perfect cunt all night until I pass out.

The feeling of waking with her in my arms is like no other. I barely let her catch her breath at all last night before I was buried balls deep inside her cunt. I finally let her sleep and managed to keep my cock out of her at dawn, though I've barely slept a wink. I slide out of bed and stare down at her naked back, just the sight of her alone has my cock hardening. I decide to let her rest and go take a shower before going in search of Luka and finding out if he was able to track the cell that text Kiara.

Twenty minutes later, I'm walking out of the pool house in a fresh suit, I had some of my things put in there in case my hunch was right. Of course, it was, Kiara is more comfortable staying out here than inside the house that robbed her of her innocence. The thought of Tony touching her has my fists clenching at my sides. I wish I could bring him back to life just so I could kill him again. I head through the back door and nod to Martha.

"Would you like your breakfast and coffee in your office, sir?" I nod and carry on. Martha has been with us for years. She practically helped raise the twins and Car, she is loyal and good at her fucking job. I leave all the hiring for household staff to her; this house wouldn't be what it is without her. I open my office door and I'm not surprised to see King, Mav and Luka already in here. I head to my chair and unbutton my jacket before claiming my seat.

"What have we got?" Luka is the first to answer me.

"They used a burner phone." *Fuck.*

"I re-checked the video surveillance from their school, I caught a partial plate number. Luka is running it through the system now." Mav seems hopeful and he's an idiot for that, a man's worst fucking enemy in this line of work is hope.

"Put word out to the other families, anyone who aides or knows of the whereabouts of my sister and doesn't tell me, will be at war with us. Bring in more men to surround the property. I want Kiara under 24/7 surveillance unless I'm with her."

"She isn't the priority here, Carlina is!" I snarl at my brother.

"You may be my underboss but you don't call the fucking shots. Carlina has been taken because he wants Kiara, that makes her a fucking priority!" King doesn't back down, it's not in his makeup.

"If anything happens to *our* sister because you are distracted by your new piece of ass—." I'm on my feet in a split second with gun out and aimed at my brother. King sits there unaffected by my show of power. He climbs to his feet slowly and holds my heated stare with one of his own.

"Speak about her like that again. I dare you," I taunt.

"One night in the sack with her and already you turn on your own family." I flinch internally at his words. King is still bitter about me killing our father. "Let me ask you this, *brother*. If a choice is to be made between *her* and our sister, who will you choose?"

Chapter Twelve

Kiara

I roll over and stretch my arm across the bed. I feel around for him but his side is cold. I slowly blink my eyes open and sigh, he's gone. I sit up and swing my legs over the side of the bed and cringe, the insides of my thighs feels sticky from his cum. My legs have bite marks and bruises from his punishing grip. Just the thought of how he took me last night and didn't give a fuck about anything aside from making me scream his name has my belly tightening and my pussy pulsing. I can still feel the ghost of his cock inside me, like he has imprinted himself on me. I need to shower! I hate the thought of washing him away but there is no way I could face the twins or King. I know I must look like I've been railed and my hair will no doubt be a mess but I don't regret a single thing about last night.

I smile to myself as I shower and relive the memories of last night. He was so attentive and caring. He may have been rough with me but I loved every second. He marked me in every way possible—he came on me, in me and all over my face. It makes me hot just thinking about how he smeared his cum all over my face then ran a finger through it only to make me suck his digit clean. It takes everything inside me not to rub my clit, I want Bishop to make me come again this morning and alleviate this ache between my thighs that the thought of him caused.

I wrap a towel around myself and head back into the bedroom to try find some clothes but screech to a halt when I see Bishop sitting on the edge of the bed with a haunted look in his eyes. I drop my towel and watch as his eyes fill with lust, then saunter over to him trying to sway my hips like a sexy bitch. I push my way between his legs and grip his hair, pulling hard enough for him to crane his neck back and look up at me. He has his hands up the backs of my thighs and doesn't stop until he is cupping my ass. I lick my lips, move and straddle his lap. I can feel he's hard for me already. I lean forward and brush my lips over his... he doesn't open for me. I pull back and furrow my brow in confusion, search his gaze and see that he fucking wants me. If that isn't enough his rock-hard cock certainly gives him away.

"I brought you some clothes. Rook is waiting outside for you." I cock my head to the side confused.

"Why is Rook waiting for me?" My heart begins beats erratically.

"He's going to take you back to school." I recoil. He grips my waist holding me still in his lap, my heart sinks as I watch a shutter fall over his eyes. He's closing himself off from me and is about turn into the Don of the Murdoch family. What a stupid fool I was to think he actually gave a shit about me. Everything he said yesterday was for nothing. He said what he did so he could get in my fucking pants, and like the stupid bitch I am, I let him. He fucked me so he could get one up on his father!

"You bastard. You used me and now that you got what you wanted, you what? Chuck me out like the trash I am?" His cold hard gaze meets mine.

"My sister comes first, always. You will return to school and once you are finished you will return here and we will marry. The videos from last night should be enough to prompt your father to return my sister and show him how in love with me you are." Tears threaten to spill at the sound of his hateful words. I shake my head denying his claim.

"You son of a bitch, don't you dare lie and turn what happened between us last night into something dirty."

"I fucked you, that's all that was. When the time comes for Carlina to be returned you will be at the meet with your father and you'll do exactly as I say or Gage will pay the price for your disobedience."

"Fuck you."

"I already broke his fucking hand, defy me again and I'll shoot out his kneecaps. Be a good girl and he may just fucking live." I slap him, my hand stings from the force of it. I push away from him and stand, not giving a fuck that I'm naked. I'm not ashamed of my body.

"You're a fucking monster. You say you will never hurt me like your father did yet, here you are... Blackmailing me by using the life of my friend to keep me in line." He slowly turns his head back to me, the fire in his eyes has me stilling. What the fuck was I thinking hitting the Don of the biggest crime family in the country? He could fucking kill me! He climbs to his feet slowly, his height and body size dwarfs me.

The look of disgust in his gaze as he stares at me has tears blurring my visions.

"You touch, look or speak to any guy while you're gone..." He reaches out and grips the back of my neck in a punishing grip until I stare up at him. I make sure he can see the hatred that I feel toward him in my eyes. "... I'll kill them in front of you and make you bathe in their blood. You think you know what I'm capable of but you don't know shit. Fuck with me, Kiara, and you will see the real beast. Tony was nothing compared to me. Get dressed and get the fuck out of my house." He releases me with a hard shove. I stumble back and hit the wall. He shoots me one last filthy look before he walks out and doesn't look back once. No sooner do I hear the door close, than I drop to my knees and sob. I'm such a fucking idiot! I wrap my arms around my legs and bury my face atop them and cry. It took Bishop mere hours to break through the walls I have built around myself to keep me safe from the hurt he just caused. I swore I would never sleep with a man unless I trusted them. I thought Gage was that but it turns out I only love him like a brother. Bishop, I've loved him since I was a child and he used that against me. He fucking knew how I felt about him and he played me like a fucking violin.

"Get up." I startle at the sound of Knight's voice. He grabs the clothes from the bed and chucks them at me whilst keeping his gaze on the wall behind me.

"W-what are you doing here?" He still won't look at me and I respect the fuck out of him for that, most guys would be getting an eyeful while they could, but not Knight.

"Rook is too soft on you. King is busy fighting his demons and Bishop, well, I guess you would rather not see that asshole right now."

"He told me to leave." The watery tone of my voice has him tensing.

"Get dressed. I'll wait out there for you." I wait until he leaves the room and closes the door behind himself, then gather myself up and climb to my feet. I have been through worse shit than this. I keep repeating that mantra in my head as I go through the motions of dressing myself. It feels good to have my own clothes again, even if they are cheap second-hand clothes. Poor Rook drove back to school, only to have to take me back today. Isn't that what I wanted though? Didn't I want to go back to school and finish my senior year and be free of this bullshit? "Hurry up." Knights clipped tone breaks me from my thoughts. I head to the door but pause and take one last look at the crumpled sheets and mess we made on the bed. I allow myself a minute to feel the anguish and pain. I finally got the guy I have always wanted, only for him to throw me away after he got what he wanted. I yank the door open and head into the living room, I cringe internally when I see Knight sitting in the same spot on the couch where Bishop made me come.

"What now?" Knight sighs and climbs to his feet. We stare at each other silently for a long while, Knight may be only seventeen but his eyes hold a wisdom no one his age should. He's probably seen more heinous things in his life than anyone twice his age.

"Now, you keep your fucking head held high as we walk through that house and past my brother. You don't let him see that he broke something inside you."

"I can't do that!" Knight's eyes flash with anger.

"You can and you will. Bishop needs to focus right now on getting my sister back, the last thing he needs is to worry that you'll go back to school and slit your wrists." I flinch at his harsh tone and shudder at the thought of doing what he said.

"I'm not fucking suicidal, Knight!"

"Good to know. Now, let's go." He brushes past me and like the sheep that I am, I follow him. The closer we get to the house, I feel my unease bleed way to anger and I latch onto that. Fuck Bishop. I lived without him and so what if he paid for my schooling, it's the least he can fucking do after what his father did to me for years. Tony may have broken my hymen but he didn't break my fucking spirit. I hold my head high and follow Knight inside, making sure to keep a mask of indifference in place as we pass by the kitchen. I spy Mav and Luka in there talking quietly. We pass the living room and just about make it past the hallway where his office is without bumping into him but of course, fate hates me. He and King exit the office and Knight stops. I keep my gaze ahead and don't bother to look at either of them. I can feel both their stares on me but I won't give him the satisfaction of looking at him. Bishop steps forward but King grips his arm stopping his movement.

"It was good to see you, princess." I scoff and turn away from them heading for the door. I hear a scuffle behind me but don't even acknowledge it. I need to get the fuck out of this house before I cry like a girl. I'm not a crier, never have been, and I refuse to start now. I wait at the bottom of the steps for Knight.

"You know he's full of shit, right?" I spin to the side and see both Gage and Rook walking toward me. I leap at Gage when he's close enough. I wrap my arms around his waist and rest my cheek against his chest. His embrace makes me feel like everything is going to be okay and that I'll make it through this thing, whatever this thing is between Bishop and I. "You okay, doll?" I pull back and smile up at him. I run my gaze over his body and that's when I see his hand, it's purple and bruised. His fingers are swollen and I can tell from the way he lifts it and holds it against his chest that it's causing him discomfort.

"I'm so sorry, Gage."

"What the hell are you sorry for? I'm the one that hid shit from you doll, not the other way around!" I place my hands on my hips and nibble on the corner of my bottom lip and shrug.

"I guess me being more pissed at Bishop lets you off the hook." A broad smile graces his face but I'm not done. "You still have a shit load of groveling to do and a lot to explain." The sound of the front door closing stops our conversation. Rook steps forward and places a hand on my shoulder.

"Good thing we have a three-hour car ride ahead of us then." I look at Rook in confusion, he rolls his eyes playfully. "Lover boy over here is coming back with us, Luka is on the wanted list so he can't guard you." I turn back to Gage.

"What about the shack?" Gage runs the fight club and I know he does other shit on the side to make money but I never asked what he did. I guess I don't need to ask now.

"Bishop had it burnt down last night, so, he's free to guard you for the rest of the year." I balk at Rook's careless tone. I know how much that place meant to Gage. I step forward and grab Gage's free hand in mine and squeeze.

"I'm so sorry," I whisper. I feel like shit knowing it's my fault this happened—all because I told Bishop I didn't want to give up fighting.

"Don't worry about it, doll. Come on, we better get going before he decides to break my other hand." I cringe. I know he meant it as a joke but still, it's way too soon to be joking about that.

Chapter Thirteen

Bishop

Two weeks

I've been getting updates about my sister every second day, always from a new number and never the same. Luka isn't able to track the calls. I've sent men to Florida to try track Anthony Bennett down, the fucker is like a ghost. He runs the show down there but no one has actually seen him. You can't even get a description of the bastard. Tony used to tell me stories about him but I thought most of them were bull-shit just to make himself feel better about not being able to take out his competition but now, I fear he may have been right.

"What if he isn't in Miami?" I look up from my laptop and stare at King.

"What do you mean?"

"Think about it, Bish. The guy is like a ghost and no one knows what he looks like. What's to say he isn't right here in New York under our fucking noses. We have caused a rift with Ramano's because you thought Car might have been with them because someone said they *thought* they saw her with Pauly."

"They are fucking bitches and everyone knows Pauly is a snitch bitch." He deserved what happened to him.

"You fucking killed the heir to the Ramano family, Bishop! They are going to clap back, it's not a matter of *if* it's a matter of *when*. We can't be fighting two wars at once!" I snap.

"What the fuck do you want me to do, King? You wanted me focused on getting Carlina back, I am fucking focused!"

"You stupid bastard. You're lashing out because you're fucking pissed that Kiara is gone! Don't think I didn't fucking know you have been sneaking up to that school every other night to spy on her!" I ball my hands into fists atop my desk.

"Tread fucking carefully, brother."

"Or what? You gonna kill me like you did Pauly? Break my hand like Gage because he dared to touch Kiara? You're fucking spiraling, B, and this time I won't be the one to pull you back." His reminder of the time I went off the rails has my anger spiking. I grip the tumbler in front of me and launch it at the wall behind King. He jumps to his feet and I do the same. I warm inside at the thought of being able to fight, I need an outlet for my anger and since fucking Kiara is off the table, beating some respect into King is second best.

"You and me, in the basement five minutes. You want to

nut up and come at me like you just did, you better be ready to back your shit up." King smiles darkly at me.

"About fucking time, get ready to have your ass handed to you, brother."

I slowly sink down onto my bed and hiss, my fucking ribs are killing me, my kidneys took a fucking beating as well. King and I went at it like wild bulls until Martha and Luka stopped us. I've never wanted to hurt my brother the way I did today. I broke my brother's fucking nose and relished in the sound of his bones breaking beneath my fist. King is my underboss and the person I trust the most in this whole world. I know deep down inside he hates me for making him choose between our family and Christine. I knew he loved her and I made him give her up so she wasn't a weakness for him.

"You good?" I rest back against the headboard and wrap my arm around my ribs and I sit up. King smirks at me from the doorway. His eyes are already turning black from his broken nose, his chest and sides are littered with angry purple bruises that match my own.

"Never better, you hit like a pussy," I snark.

"Your sluggish movements would disagree with you, brother." I sigh and decide to ask him the question that has been eating away at me since she walked out two weeks ago.

"Did you tell me I had to get rid of her because I did the same thing to you?" King looks shocked by my question.

"No, I told you to pull your head out of her cunt and focus on our sister. Kiara has always been a blind spot for you. You fucking lost it after she went missing, Bishop. You may not want to admit it to yourself but you have been in

love with that girl since she was fifteen. Kiara may be a
Bennett but that doesn't mean you have to marry her
because of that. Fuck what Tony wanted, Bish. He's dead."
His words hit their mark. I know what he says is true but I
can't go down that road right now. I sent her away with my
brothers and fucking Gage, no less. I know he is in love with
her but I also know she doesn't feel the same way about him.
I go out and watch her every other day, just being near her
calms the beast inside me that thirsts for blood. I went nuts
when she disappeared, I searched for her daily, I found her
mother and pressed her for information. The bitch was so
strung out she didn't even know what fucking day it was.

"What if her father does have Carlina, what do we do
then?"

"We get our sister back."

"At what cost? Are you really willing to trade Kiara for
Carlina?" I want to say yes, it should be an easy choice. But
a part of me knows I would never let Kiara go, when I found
her with Gage, I knew I could control her moves from afar
and allow her the illusion of freedom. She has no idea how I
know Gage and no doubt he will fill her in while they are at
school, he was supposed to keep her safe until I dealt with
Tony. When I found the videos, what that sick fuck had
done to not only Kiara but my sister as well, I lost it and
killed him that same day. She doesn't need to tell me about
what happened, I've seen it for myself and the sight made
me sick. It happened just down the hall from me and I had
no fucking idea. I never recorded her and I in the pool
house, I let her believe I did so she would leave. Tony had
been sending the videos of what he was doing to her to her
father, that is the only reason he hasn't come for her.

"I don't know." I feel like a bastard for saying that out
loud but I won't lie to King.

"We'll figure it out, Bish, we always do. You need to get your head on straight and focus on what is at stake here, I won't risk our sister's life, not even for Kiara." I nod. "You're the leader of this family, Bishop. Our other businesses have suffered since Kiara started school, your obsession with her has clouded your judgment."

"You have my word, as of tomorrow I will be focused on returning our family to its former standing."

Chapter Fourteen

Kiara

I walk aimlessly to my last class. I've just been existing these past two weeks. I haven't tasted the food I consume or even smelt a single thing. It's as if Bishop has ruined me for the rest of the world. He was always an enigma, someone for me to fantasize about as I grew up. He was the unobtainable boy that I always wanted but knew I could never have. We come from two totally different worlds. The only time I ever ate was at his house, he never had to worry about when his next meal would be, I did. I wear second hand clothes from the thrift store, he wears designer suits. I catch the bus, he drives a fucking Tesla! I thought with him finally admitting his feelings and how he watched me, I would finally land the guy of my dreams. How wrong was I? I drop down in my seat next to Quinn, he smiles kindly at me and I try to do the same, but judging from how he grimaces I fail.

"You okay? You seem a bit off lately." I sigh and slump down in my chair as Mr. Rogers begins his boring ass history lesson.

"Just got a lot of shit going on," I mutter quietly. Quinn chuckles and wraps an arm around my shoulder shaking me.

"You getting all lonely in your room since Car is away traveling?" The twins have told everyone that their sister is on a trip in Europe to pamper herself, it's their belated birthday present to her. The truth is, yes, it is fucking hard staying in that room alone every night. I hate that she is missing and no one knows if she's okay or if they have fucking hurt her. I want to text the number on my phone that sends pictures of her every other day but I'm not deluded enough to think Bishop hasn't got Luka monitoring my phone or if he has even mirrored it.

"No, my room is fine," I force out.

"Well, if you ever want company, you got my number." I know Quinn is joking and means well but the last thing I need right now is to have a guy hanging around me. Gage is sporting a cast because he got close to me and I would never forgive myself if Quinn got hurt because of me. I untangle myself from him and turn to smile politely not wanting to hurt his feelings but I find his gaze fixed ahead. It's then I notice how silent the room is. A shiver travels down my spine and I immediately turn toward the front of the room. Mr. Rogers stares toward the door way, I follow his line of sight and freeze. Standing in the doorway like he owns the fucking school is none other than Bishop Murdoch. I hate that my eyes drink in every inch of him, the way his suit hugs his body and the way his muscles bulge in his jacket or the way his slacks fit his muscular legs perfectly. His brown eyes hold an intensity that has me wanting to cower beneath my desk. his hair is slicked back against his head, I watch as gaze shifts slightly and I follow it.

Fuck!

I drop my hold on Quinn's arm, scramble to my feet and quickly grab my books before shoving them in my bag. I ignore his curious gaze and question as to who the fuck Bishop is. I keep my head down as I make my way toward the front of the class, wanting to rip those cheer bitches' eyes out. They sit in the front row pushing their chests out and batting their lashes hoping Bishop will fuck them or at the very least give them a pity fuck. I sling my bag over my shoulder and stop an inch in front of him, he doesn't say a word as he grips my hand and leads me from the room. The feeling of my hand inside his sends a thrill through me, I want to hate him so badly, my mind does hate him but my heart doesn't.

Stupid fucking heart!

I practically have to jog to keep up with his long ass legs, when I stumble the second time he grinds to a halt and growls before spinning around and hoisting me over his shoulder. My bag slides off and I try to catch it but lands on the ground.

"Bishop, my bag!" He curses before spinning around and picking it up. He marches us out of the building and I cringe when I hear pelts of laughter from students as he carries me across the quad and heads toward the dorms. I don't even bother to fight or try to free myself from his hold, all it would do is piss him off and I'm not up to that argument right now. I'll wait till we are behind closed doors, then let him have a piece of my mind. We stop at the doors to the dorms and I scoff when I hear him entering the code, of course he fucking knows what the code to the girls dorms is. He bypasses the elevators and takes the stairs, how he is climbing with me on his shoulder and not puffing or slowing down amazes the fuck out of me.

When we hit my floor, he kicks the door open and continues down the hall until he reaches mine and Car's room. He pulls a key from his pocket electing an eye roll from me, I'm not even surprised he has his own freaking key! He waltzes inside like he owns the fucking place, for all I know he probably fucking does! He kicks the door shut then in one swift move he yanks me from his shoulder, then I'm pressed against the door by his hulking frame. His eyes burn with unbridled rage as he stares down at me. I return his heated glare with one of my own. He does not get to throw me away and then come back here like he fucking owns me, he said I had till graduation before I had to go back and marry his bossy ass.

"I fucking warned you about what would happen." I furrow my brow confused as fuck. He pulls his phone from his pocket and dials someone. After a minute whoever it is picks up. "Back row, second chair from the end. Deal with it." He ends the call and I mull over his words until it sinks in.

"That's Quinn's chair! Don't you fucking hurt him, Bishop. I mean it!" He slams his hands either side of my head caging me in. I push against his chest but of course the bastard doesn't even budge. He bends until we are eye to eye, I make sure he can see the anger in my eyes.

"I warned you what would happen if you looked, touched or spoke to anyone else—."

"Oh, fuck right off with that shit!" His eyes twitch in anger but I push on. "You kicked *me* out, not the fucking other way around. You don't get to tell me what the fuck to do. You said I had until graduation before I had to marry your overbearing ass. If I want to fuck my way through the football team until then, I will." No sooner have the words left my mouth does his hand wrap around my throat, his grip is so tight I gasp for air and claw at his arm trying to push him. I swing out and land a right hook to his jaw, all that does is serve to piss him off more! I start to get light headed and know I only have a few seconds before I pass out. I lash out and kick him straight in the dick! He goes down like a sack of shit, I gasp and suck in as much air as I can before I quickly dart around him, he catches my ankle and I fall forward only managing to catch myself at the last second before I headbutt the floor. I kick out and manage to land a kick and try to crawl away but he's on me before I can move an inch, he flips me onto my back and straddles me effectively using his weight against me, I try to punch him again but he pins my arms above my head.

"Hit me again—."

"And what? You'll fuck me? Break my hand or shoot out Gage's kneecaps? Which one is it this time, Bishop?" He grips both my hands in his one and then grips my chin with the other, his grip is punishing but I refuse to give him the satisfaction of whimpering.

"I'll fuck you whenever and wherever I want."

"Try it and I'll bite your fucking dick off, asshole."

"Baby, your dirty talk turns me the fuck on." To drive his point home, he grinds against me and I stifle the shocked gasp that wants to break free when I feel his hardness against my stomach.

"You're sick." I wrench my head to the side unable to look at him, he chuckles and it pisses me the fuck off. I'm about to rip him a new asshole but freeze when he bends down and runs his nose along the column of my neck up to my ear. He nibbles on my lobe and I'm beyond disgusted in myself when a moan breaks free as he sucks it into his mouth. He releases my lobe and licks his way along my jaw, my body begs for me to give in and face him so he can kiss me but my mind knows better. Bishop is a master manipulator and played me like a fool last time, but I won't fall for that again.

"I want to fuck you." I scoff but still refuse to meet his stare.

"Go find one of the cheer bitches and fuck them, they would be happy to let you blow your load on their faces." He pulls back and grips my chin roughly, turning me back to face him. I make sure I keep my emotions in check and don't let him see that even saying that out loud has a pang hitting me square in the chest at the thought of him with someone else.

"That what you want? You want me to go fuck one of those blow-up dolls, then come back here so you can lick their cum off my cock?" I fight the flinch that wants to break free but fail. The victorious smirk that graces his handsome face pisses me off. "Tell me. If you don't, I'll go back and get that red head that was sitting in the front row." Tears build behind my eyes, I will them to stay put but one lone tear slips free. Bishop trails it movement before leaning down and catching it on his tongue which draws a whimper from me.

"Get off me." I sound defeated and I hate it, but right now I don't care. I just want him to go and stay the hell away from me. One night with him nearly destroyed me. It sounds so pathetic but if you've been in love with someone your whole life and finally get them for a night, it fucking shatters you when they push you away and act like you mean nothing to them. "Please," I whisper. He leans back and stares down at me with an unreadable expression on his face.

"Do you really think I would do that to you?"

"What?"

"Go fuck some slut, then crawl in bed next to you?" I gape at him, is he fucking delusional?

"I don't even know you anymore, Bishop. So, yeah, I do think you would do something as fucking low as that because you made it crystal fucking clear I mean nothing to you. If you're only here because you want your dick wet, fuck me, then go. I mean it's not like guys in your family are used to the word no from a female."

Chapter Fifteen

Bishop

I leap off her like she burnt me, staring down at her, utterly sickened by what she just said. She pushes herself into a sitting position but makes no move to stand, she grips her stained gray tee and pulls it over head exposing her cotton bra, she reaches behind to unclasp it but I look away.

"Put your fucking shirt back on." She scoffs and I watch from the corner of my eye as she grabs her shirt, stands and the heads toward her bed. I turn back toward her and watch as she pops the button on her jeans and then slides them down her legs, I avert my gaze to the ceiling. "What the fuck are you doing?"

"Clearly you're not here to fuck me so, I'm going to take a fucking shower before I have to listen to you rant about whatever it is that you came here to say." That gets my attention, I return my stare to her and grind my teeth.

"I've killed men for less——."

"If you don't like the way I talk to you, get your gun and shoot me or just fucking leave, I don't care anymore, Bishop." The anger in her eyes melts away and is replaced by resignation. "My life isn't my own and never was, so do whatever it is you have to do because I give up, you win, okay?" I open my mouth to deny her claim but snap it shut when she drops her panties and unclasps her bra, her tits and pussy are on full display. My cock pushes against the confines of my boxers begging me to sink inside her but I won't. Not after what she just said. She heads toward me and I jump out of the way. I watch her hips sway side to side and love the way her plump ass jiggles as she heads toward the bathroom. I bite my lip and war within myself whether or not I should join her or leave her cool off.

Fuck it.

I follow after her and fight my smirk when she squeals at the sight of me in her tiny as fuck bathroom. I find it comical that after stripping in front of me she now tries to hide her tits and pussy behind her arms. I've tasted every inch of her and know her body better than she probably does. I size up her shower and groan internally. It's too fucking small for me to fit in there with her.

"Get the fuck out!"

"I've ate your cunt and had your cum dripping down my chin." I smirk when I see a blush slowly rise to her cheeks.

"Yeah, well, that was a one-night thing and it won't be happening again so, get the fuck out." I smirk cockily at her and watch as her face contorts. "I mean it, Bishop."

"You don't mean shit, I bet you if I put a finger inside

your tight cunt you'd be wet as fuck for me." Her mouth opens slightly. I turn and leave her to stew in her anger while I wait for her on her bed. Five minutes later she walks out with a towel wrapped around her head and one around her body. She shoots me a glare when she spots me on her bed, I smile. She huffs and stomps over to her dresser, pulling open her drawer and grabbing a pair of red satin panties. I grit my teeth to stop the groan from slipping out. She turns her back to me and drops the towel as she pulls them on. They ride high enough to show off the bottom of her ass cheeks. I shift on her bed and try to adjust my cock. She opens another drawer, pulls out a shirt and slips it on. I narrow my eyes at it—it's too big to be her own as it stops just above her knees. I jump to my feet and spin her around to face me, then bend so we are nose to nose. "Whose fucking shirt are you wearing?" Her brows raise as she leans forward and ghosts her lips over mine as she speaks.

"Rook's." I see red, grip the shirt the collar and tear it right down the middle before yanking it off her and chuck it to the side. "You asshole! I liked that shirt!"

"I don't give a fuck!" She scrunches her face in anger before turning to her drawer and pulling out another plain black tee. Just as she's about to slip it on I yank it away from her and hold it above my head.

"Whose is this one?" She doesn't answer and tries to jump for it. My anger dissipates as I watch her full tits bounce in front of me.

"Give it to me." I hold it a bit lower and bite my lip to stop the smile breaking free when she jumps again. I want to fucking suck on her tits and listen to the sounds she makes as I bite down on her nipple. "Bishop!" The sound of my name pulls me from my thoughts.

"What?"

"Can I have the shirt?" I narrow my eyes at her as I grip it between my hands ready to tear it in half. "Stop!"

"Why?"

"Because it's your shirt! And so was the fucking other one you just ripped." I drop my arm back to my side and stare at her blankly. She drops her gaze to the floor in embarrassment.

"You have my shirts?" She releases a loud breath and nods. "Why?" She remains silent and scuffs her toes on the carpet. Tired of waiting for her reply, I grip her chin and lift her face to mine. "Why do you have my shirts?"

"Rook packed my clothes that I wore to your house. He thought I might want something... that reminded me of you," she whispers the last part. Hearing those words from her mouth have something inside me fracturing. All thought flees me as I drop the shirt and cup her face between my hands, swipe my thumbs over her cheeks and search her eyes for any sign that she wants me to stop. When I don't see one, I close the space between us and kiss her. She opens for me instantly and I groan at the taste of her. She reaches up and wraps her arms around my neck, deepening the kiss. I run my hands down her sides and love how she shivers from my touch. I grip the globes of her ass and lift her, making her wrap her legs around me and moan when she feels my cock pressed against her. I turn us toward her bed ready to lay her down and fucking ravish every inch of her body but she pulls back and breaks our kiss. "We can't." I sigh and nod my head, then place her on the edge of her bed before retrieving the shirt from the floor and handing it to her.

I drop down on the side of my sister's bed and watch her shuffle backward and cross her legs under herself. From where I'm sitting, I have a perfect view between her legs of her red panties. I push thoughts of fucking her out of my head and focus on the reason why I came here today. I don't know how much the twins have told her but from how shocked she was to see me I'm guessing they have been keeping her in dark.

"I'm sorry." I lift my gaze to hers in shock.

"Sorry for what?" She sighs and runs a hand through her long black hair, I want to reach out and pull on the strands just the way she likes, but I refrain.

"For saying what I said. That wasn't fair of me and it was wrong." I stare at her like an idiot for a beat... She is apologizing to me for saying something that is actually true, when I'm the one who treated her like a whore. This girl is fucking something else, that is for sure.

"You have nothing to be sorry about. What Tony did to you..." I shake my head and try to tamper the rage inside me. Every time I think about what he did to her and Car I want to fucking kill him all over again.

"It wasn't you, Bishop. Your father did that to me and I'm... dealing with it."

"You shouldn't have to!" I snap. She sighs as her shoulders slump forward, I hate how defeated she looks. For the past two weeks I have snuck in here and hidden in the shadows as I watched her sleep. Knight removed the fucking cameras in here under King's orders, so I had no other choice but to come here just so I could see her. I hate to admit it but King made a good call. I would have spent hours watching her instead of dealing with the shit I had to, which is the reason I'm here.

"Why did you come here today?" Her pale blue eyes plead with me to speak the truth.

"I need you to make a call." She eyes me suspiciously for a moment before speaking.

"If you came all this way for me to call Gage—"

"I'm not here for that bastard."

"Then who?" I hold her gaze as I deliver the blow that I know is going to set her off like the Fourth of July.

"I need you to call your father."

Chapter Sixteen

Kiara

He must have lost his goddam mind!

There is no fucking way in hell I am making that call. Bishop can suck a fat dick if he thinks I'm going to do that. I climb off the bed and begin to pace the room trying to calm myself down. I stop every couple of minutes to yell at him but at the sight of him reclined on Car's pink bed I think better of it. Time ticks by as I try to formulate a response to such a stupid as fuck question!

"You're going to ruin the carpet." I glare at him over my shoulder and bare my teeth, the bastard has the audacity to laugh at me.

"This is not funny! You come here and demand this of me after treating me like shit the last time I saw you. You think that just because the sight of you makes me weak in the knees that I'll do as you say? Get fucking real, Bishop. You may have a magic dick that makes me speak in tongues but even your cock can't make me call that asshole."

"Want to make a bet?" I scrunch my face in confusion. "A bet?"

"That my cock can make you call him." I throw my hands up in frustration, I'm still so fucking angry at him for how he treated me. Yet having him so close to me clouds my fucking rational thought. I need to get the fuck out this room and away from Bishop before I do something dumb, like call my father. I march over to my bag, grab my phone and keys, then head for the door. I grip the handle and open it just a smidge before it's slammed shut, his hand resting just above my head. I spin around to face him placing my hands on my hips. "Where the fuck do you think you're going dressed like that?" My anger boils over.

"To find Gage—" I don't even get to finish my sentence before his hand is around my throat and pushing me flush against the door. His hold isn't punishing this time but it's tight enough to let me know he is pissed.

"You're playing with his life here, baby. You keep throwing that little bitch in my face every time we have a spat and I'm just about done with it."

"He's my best friend!"

"You fuck all your best friends?"

"Nope." He relaxes slightly but I'm not done taunting him, I want to hurt him the way he hurt me. "Just him." His grip tightens and I don't bother to fight him, it's no use. He gets right in my face, his scent surrounding me and making me dizzy. He pulls his phone out and turns it to me as he unlocks it. My mouth drops open when I see his screensaver. He pulls up Knight's number but before he can push call, I snatch it from him and return to his home screen and stare. He reaches for it but I move it out of his reach and turn it toward him. "Why am I your screensaver?" It's a picture of me sitting under the tree in the quad laughing at something. It's a grainy picture, so I know he has zoomed in and cropped whoever was with me out. He snatches his phone from me and pockets it as he steps back releasing his hold on me. "I'm starting to think you choking me is your way of kissing me hello." That earns me a glare from him as he heads toward my desk and drops into my chair. I remain where I am as I ask him again, "Why am I your screensaver and how the fuck did you get that picture, Bishop?"

"Because I like to look at you." I hate that his words have me feeling all warm and shit inside.

"How did you get that picture?" He leans forward and rests his arms on his legs and looks up at me. For the first time today he doesn't shield his emotions from me.

"I took it the second week you started school here." That surprises the fuck out of me.

"You came up here to see your siblings?" He shakes his head.

"I came to see you." My mouth drops open and my eyes widen in surprise.

"Do... do you do that often? Come to see me, I mean?" I wait with bated breath for him to answer me. A part of me wants him to say yes but the other part of me, that is pissed as hell at him, wants him to deny me.

"Ever since the day you left, I come up here every second night and sit right here and watch you sleep like a fucking addict. You're a fucking addiction to me, Kiara, and I can never get enough of you. Since the moment you started school here you have become my obsession. I can't focus, I barely sleep and I can't even run my companies because all I think about every fucking minute of every day is you!" His admission has all the anger inside me dissipating. I make my way toward him and sit on the end of my bed, a few inches of space separate us.

"Why did you say all of those things to me at your house?"

"I lied."

"Why should I believe you? You told me everything I wanted to hear and I gave you my body, only for you to turn around and spit on it the next day." He drops his gaze to the floor and intertwines his fingers between his legs. I wait for him to answer. I need to hear his reasoning as to why he broke my fucking heart. He destroyed me with his callous words. The way he spoke to me made me feel like I was nothing more than shit beneath his shoe.

"I had to say those things so you would leave. I never meant any of it, you have to know that. Kiara, you mean... so much to me and King thought it was best—"

"King? That was King's fucking idea?" I seethe. He meets my gaze and the sheepish look in his eyes does nothing to ease the rage brewing inside me.

"He thought it was better if I wasn't distracted—"

"Give me your phone."

"What, why?"

"Give me your fucking phone, Bishop." He pulls it out and unlocks it for me before handing it over. I scroll through his contacts until I find King's number. I hit dial and wait for the piece of shit to answer. Bishops stares at me like I'm an alien but I ignore him. King finally answers after the fourth ring.

"What's up, Bish?"

"You little bitch! You fucking wait till I see you. You're no fucking king! You're a weak-ass pawn and I'm the motherfucking queen who just put your ass in checkmate, you little bitch!" I scream. Bishop rolls his lips over his teeth, to try stop his smile from breaking free. I pin him with a dirty look that has him turning away from me.

"Princess, it's good to hear from you."

"I'm going to chop your fucking cock off and break your fucking nose! How dare you call me a fucking distraction—" King cuts me off mid rant.

"You are!" He shouts. "Where the fuck is Bishop now, Kiara? Not here where he fucking should be, smoothing things over with Ramano family. He's too busy trying to bury his fucking dick between your legs instead of being the Don of this fucking family. My sister is still missing and he's too much of pussy to trade you for her." Bishop snatches the phone from me and ignores my protests as he holds it to his ear. I try to yank it back but he snakes out his hand, places it over my mouth and pushes me back till I'm flat against the bed.

"You ever, and I mean *ever*, speak to her like that again, brother or not, I will fucking kill you." I can't hear King's reply no matter how much I try. I squirm beneath his hold and smack his chest but he just ignores me. "Sort it out. Call me when it's done and don't fuck it up." He ends the call and places the phone in his pocket, taking his sweet ass time like he isn't holding me captive with one fucking hand. Having had enough of being subdued, I dart my tongue out and lick his palm. He snaps his gaze down to me and when I see the lust lurking in the depths of his brown eyes, I close my mouth and quit moving. "Now, if I remove my hand are you going to be a good girl or do I need to shove something else in it to make you more compliant?" I shake my head and he slowly removes his hand.

Bishop and I haven't said a word to each other since I rang King. He ordered us Chinese takeout and had Mav deliver it to my room. I was shocked as fuck when he walked back in with the takeout and an overnight bag. I kept quiet and didn't say a word. He plated up the food on the plates Car had stashed in our room. I sit here nibbling on my food, doing my homework on my bed as Bishop sits at my desk eating his food and typing away on his laptop Mav brought him. I'm nearly finished my English assignment when he stands, grabs his bag and heads toward the bathroom. I zone out for a while until he returns from the bathroom and sits back at my desk. I don't even pay him any attention until I finish my work and close my book. I look up and freeze.

Holy mother mercy!

Bishop sits at my desk shirtless and in a pair of gray fucking sweatpants! My wet dream has come true, he looks like a fucking snack. I dart my tongue out to moisten my lips as I drink in the sight of him. All his tattoos are on display and the sight of his coiled muscles make me fucking wet and near on panting. He closes the lid on his laptop and gathers up his plate, turns to place it in the trash and I screech loudly. He spins around to face me, searching my face for what has caused me to react that way.

"What happened?" I open and close my mouth a few times, unable to formulate words. "Kiara?" The sound of my name has me snapping out of my stupor.

"Your tattoo." His forehead creases.

"Yeah, what about them?"

"Don't fucking play coy. You know which *one* I'm talking about." He shrugs his shoulders like I'm making a big deal out of nothing. He dumps his plate, then returns to grab mine, all the while I just sit here staring at him. He comes back and stands in front of me. I push up from my stomach and rest back on my haunches as I gaze up at him. "Bishop."

"Kiara."

"Don't patronize me." He sighs and runs a hand through his hair.

"I'm tired, can we fight about this tomorrow?" I swipe my books off the bed and crawl toward him on my knees, reach out and grip his waist.

"I don't want to fight with you, can I just see it... Please?" A tired sigh escapes him as he turns in my hold. I stretch up on my knees and trace my finger over the tattoo between his shoulder blades. I bite my lip as I trace each letter. He shudders under my touch.

Kiara.

I trace the letters of my name a couple times before he finally steps out of reach and turns to face me. I hate the look of uncertainty in his eyes but I don't know what to say. He has my fucking name tattooed on his back—that shit isn't coming off in the shower! I look at him and for the first time I see it in his eyes, he really does care about me. I stand up from the bed and close the space between us, grab his hand and pull him toward the bed. I push him down so he is sitting on the edge, then climb atop his lap. He grips my waist instantly. I cup his face between my hands and don't overthink it as I kiss him. His hold on my waist tightens as his tongue invades my mouth. I moan at the taste of him. The sight of him in a pair of sweats and seeing my name across his back has me hot and needy, needing him to soothe the ache he caused between my thighs. I grind down against his cock and love the groan that comes from him. He grips the bottom of my shirt and lifts it up, breaking our kiss so he can chuck it to the side. He cups both of my tits in his hands and runs his thumbs over my nipples, pulling a moan from me.

"I want to draw this out but I need to be inside you, baby. Can I fuck you?" My heart soars at the fact he is asking me and not just flipping me on my back taking control like I know he wants to. Instead of using words I push against his chest until he is lying flat on his back, shimmy off his lap and grip the waistband of his sweats, then pull them down. He rests up on his elbows and smirks at me.

"No boxers?" He shrugs boyishly and that draws a smile from me.

"I wanted you to have easy access to my cock." I shake my head as I slide my panties down my legs and step out of them. His heated stare follows every one of my movements. I straddle his lap and grip his cock lining it up with my entrance, then slowly sink down onto him and moan. I lower myself slowly giving my body time to adjust but Bishop has other ideas, he sits forward grips my hips and slams me down on his cock. I scream out and quickly clamp my mouth closed, trying to stay quiet. "I want to hear you scream my fucking name, baby." I shake my head.

"No, you're not supposed to be here after curfew." He smirks and thrusts up inside me causing me to cry out again. I smack my hand over my mouth but he rips it away. "Bishop, I'll get kicked out." He grips my hair and yanks my head back, exposing my neck to him and sucks on the side causing me to moan when he bites on my flesh. Fuck it, I grind down on him and he releases his bite on my neck to groan, then grips my hips and leans back. I brace my hands on his chest as I bounce up and down on his cock, biting my lip to keep myself from crying out. Sweat beads my brow and I'm so fucking horny that I know it won't be long before I come.

"Stop fucking staying quiet, Kiara." I shake my head as I continue to ride him, chasing my climax. "If you come and don't scream my fucking name, you'll be sucking my cock for the next month and I won't fuck you."

"Oh God, I can't," I manage say before I bite my lip again.

"I own the fucking school. I'll fire the bastard that tries to kick you out. Now fucking ride my cock and come all over it so I can eat your fucking cunt and taste you." Oh God, his words spur me on. I ride him hard and fast, moving my legs up and rising up on the balls of my feet so I can squat up and down on his cock. "Fuck, baby. Just like that." I slam down on his cock twice more before I shatter above him screaming his fucking name. He grips my waist and pushes me off him. I drop to the floor and climb to my knees when he stands, lock my arms behind my back and open my mouth. He slams his cock inside my mouth causing me to gag, then grips the back of my hair and fucks my face so hard I feel my jaw click. I moan at the taste of my cum on his cock. Right as I'm getting into sucking him off, he pulls out and yanks on my hair until I stand, then pushes me over the side of Carlina's bed, kicks my legs apart and slams into me from behind.

"Holy fuck."

"Take every fucking inch of my cock, baby."

"Yes, fuck me just like that and make me come again!" His grip on my waist is bruising but I love the fucking pain. He fucks me so hard and deep that when I come again, I almost fucking black out. He slams into me two more times before I feel his hot cum shoot inside me. He cries out my name and fuck does the sound of him losing control and screaming my name do things to my insides. There is no way I'll be able to walk away from him again after seeing my name on his back and especially not after the way he just fucked me. I'm going to be walking bowlegged tomorrow.

Chapter Seventeen

Bishop

I nuzzle into the side of her neck and savior this moment—
waking up next to her has to be on my list of the top five
best moments of my life. She stirs and I smile against her
neck. I know she must be sore and as much as I want to fuck
her again, I need to get ready to head home and handle shit
with the Ramano family. Victor is getting antsy and King
isn't able to handle it without me. She rolls over and blinks
her eyes open slowly, smiling.

"I thought you would be gone." I place a quick kiss to
her lips before answering.

"Nah, I thought I'd walk you to class before I left." She
hums her approval and stretches, the blanket sliding down
her chest and exposing her tits. They're covered in hickeys
and I fucking love knowing my brand will be on her for

days. I want every motherfucker here to know she belongs to me and if they even so much as think about touching what is mine, I'll kill them.

"Okay, do I have time for a shower?"

"Yeah, baby." I slip out of the bed and help her up, running my gaze over her and see the bruises that mark her hips from my punishing hold. I should feel bad about it but I don't. I fucking love handling her rough and I know she does too. She slips past me and pauses just before going into the shower, a look of unease crossing her face. "What's wrong?"

"Did you really video us last time?" I blow out a breath and run my hand through my hair as I shake my head.

"I would never use you like that. I only said it—"

"To be a dick?" I glare at her but nod. "Are you still going to be nice to me when I get out of the shower or are you going to kick me out again?"

"Well, this is your room so you would be the one kicking me out." She stares at me with a bored look. "I'll still be here and happy to see you, okay?" She nods and turns away but pauses before slowly turning back to fully face me. She nibbles on her bottom lip which I now know is a nervous gesture of hers. "Say whatever it is you need to say, baby."

"Did you fuck me last night so I would call my father?" Fuck, I close the space between us, grip her face between my hands and lift it until she is looking in my eyes.

"No. I fucked you all night long because I couldn't get enough of being inside your tight cunt." Heat begins to rise in her cheeks at my crass words, but it's the truth, her pussy is like a fucking drug to me.

"Do... do you still want me to call him?" I drop my hold on her and step back, scrub a hand down my face and realize now, in this moment, King is right. The thought of hurting her is clouding my judgment. Anthony was clear in his last message, only Kiara was to call or we would receive pieces of our sister in the mail. With that thought in mind I push my feelings for her aside and channel my inner beast that thirsts for the blood of his enemies.

"Yes. If you don't make the call, he'll start sending pieces of Carlina's body to us and I won't have that." To my surprise she nods.

"Okay, can I do it after class today?" I want to say no and tell her to do it now but I need Luka here with me to trace the call and King on standby in case we get a ping on his location.

"Yeah, shower and I'll take you to class. I'll come back tonight and you can do it." A broad smile stretches across her face. I eye her warily. "Why are you smiling at me?" She shrugs and heads toward the shower, calling back over her shoulder before closing the door,

"Sleeping over again, someone might think you're pussy whipped." She closes the door and I mutter to myself.

"Yeah, I fucking am."

After Kiara and I are both showered and changed, I led her from her dorm with her hand in mine. People stare as we pass by but I'm used to the curious looks. I peer down at Kiara from behind my sunglasses and find she is looking down at her feet as we cross the quad. I hate that she feels inferior because she wasn't raised with a trust fund like these assholes. It wouldn't matter if one of these bitches had all the money in the world, money means nothing to me.

"Why do you let their stares bother you?" She looks up

at me as we continue toward the cafeteria where she wants to get a coffee and breakfast.

"They don't bother me."

"Don't bullshit me, Kiara," I snap. She releases a whoosh of air before looking straight ahead as she answers.

"They're not staring at me, Bishop. They're staring at you and wondering why you're walking your whore to breakfast." I stop and yank her to a stop. She stumbles backward and I grip her waist making her face me. She eyes me warily as I lift my glasses and place them on my head so she can see the look in my eyes.

"Don't ever, I mean ever, fucking call yourself a whore again," I grit out, my anger soaring inside me at the way she views herself.

"I'm the daughter of one."

"You are not your mother. Fuck what these entitled pricks think." I can tell she doesn't believe a word I'm saying and that pisses me off. I grip her chin and tilt her face up before smashing my lips against hers. She melts into me like I knew she would, I don't like public displays of affection but if this is what it takes to make her feel better and surer about us, then I'll do it. I pull back and smile down at her when I see the want in her eyes. She groans and bats my hand away.

"Now, I want to fuck." I throw my head back and laugh. She is the light I never knew I needed in my life. Kiara Bennett is repairing the damage inside me and she doesn't even have to try.

We get her coffee and breakfast before walking back outside to the tree I know she sits under everyday with my brothers and their friends. She stares at me like I've lost my mind when I drop to the ground and lean against the tree. "Bishop, what the fuck?" I stare up at her slightly confused.

"What?"

"You're wearing thousands of dollars and you just fucking plop on the ground like its nothing." I can't help the laugh that burst out of me, only she would think about me ruining my suit. I part my legs and flick my gaze to my lap. She rolls her eyes before sitting between my legs. I wrap my arms around her waist and rest my chin on her shoulder. I grind my teeth when I see the twins and some of their other friends walking toward us. The redhaired cheerleader and a couple of other girls walk with them. Kiara lifts her head and when she spots the girls she snorts.

"What's wrong, don't like them?" I whisper.

"Those bitches are only coming over because you're here." I smirk.

"Jealous, are we?" She scoffs but doesn't respond. Rook smiles widely as he drops down with his tray. Knight just nods. The guys stand there awkwardly, the four sluts bat their lashes and push out their chests whilst staring at me. Fucking hell, when did high school girls become so fucking bold? Their desperation isn't a good fucking look.

"Guys, sit." They do as Kiara says and I sneer at the bastard that had his hands on her yesterday. Rook laughs and it pisses me off. He stopped Mav from beating the shit out of his team mate and he'll fucking pay for that.

"Not gonna introduce us to your... friend?" Kiara scoffs at the redhead bitch.

"Nope." She pops the '*p*'.

"Well, that is just rude!" the blonde one snips. Knight shoots them a glare but they ignore him. "I'm Stacey," she singsongs, the sound of her nasally voice annoys the shit out of me.

"And he doesn't give a fuck, now beat your feet and

fuck off." I fight the smirk that wants to break free at Rook's blatant dismissal of them. The stupid airheads just giggle.

"I'm Lana," the brown-haired dipsy looking one says. I remain silent and tighten my hold on Kiara, I can feel how tense she is and a part of me loves the fact that she is pissed off at these girls for talking to me. Now she knows what it fucking feels like.

"You should come watch us practice," Lana says as she flutters her fake lashes at me.

"And you four should get the fuck out of here before I break your fake-ass noses!" Knight, Rook and the rest of the guy's whistle and let out a chorus of *oh shits*. The four girls glare down at Kiara like she is nothing but trash beneath their shoe and it pisses me off.

"I'm sure he would rather spend time with a real woman then some wannabe hobo like you!" I feel her flinch even though she tries to hide it. I'm done with this shit! I grab her chin and pull her face to the side, ignoring the look of hurt in her eyes as I kiss her long and hard. She melts against me. I break the kiss and turn back to face the bitches ready to tear their asses down a peg. I climb to my feet and keep my gaze on them as I step around Kiara and straighten out my suit. Knight and Rook flank either side of me as I close the space between the girls and me. They smile brightly like they have just won but these bitches know nothing. They will not get away with treating my girl like that! "I thought you would come to your senses," Lana snarks. I smile invitingly and watch as they relax slightly.

"Oh, I came, don't you worry about that." They cover their mouths and giggle. They think I'm about to proposition them.

"I bet we could do it better than the likes of that trash," the redhead bitch snarls. I don't even look at Kiara.

"Call my fiancée trash again and I'll have your asses banned from the squad and kicked out of this fucking school." The blonde opens her mouth but I carry on. "You so much as make a snide remark or even look at her wrong, your asses will be out!"

"You can't do that!" Stacey pipes up. I chuckle but there is no humor to it.

"I own the fucking school you dense mutt. Test me again and I won't hold her back from breaking your fucking faces." I leave them to wallow in their stupor as I turn back to my girl. She stares up at me with wonder and amazement in her eyes, her mouth slack with her shock. "See you tonight, baby." She snaps her mouth closed and nods.

Chapter Eighteen

Kiara

I walk out of last period and I'm disappointed that Bishop isn't waiting for me. I shake off my unease when I push through the doors and see Gage standing at the bottom of the steps. I smile wide and race toward him, wrap my arms around him and relish in the comfort his embrace brings me. He laughs but returns my hug. We pull apart and he nods his head for me to follow him. We walk side by side toward my dorm in silence. I can tell there is something eating away at him, so I veer to the left and claim one of the bench seats outside my dorm.

"What's on your mind?" I ask as we sit down. Students pass us in a world of their own, laughing and talking amongst themselves. Gage faces me and I can see the torment in his eyes, it has me on edge. "Gage?" I prompt.

"Doll, there is something you need to know."

"What?" He darts his gaze around as if making sure that no one is listening to us.

"Bishop had your phone mirrored." I roll my eyes.

"Yeah, I figured. That's why I haven't been texting you." Shame washes over me at the fact I shut my best friend out because of a guy.

"It's not that." I cock my head to the side confused.

"What is it then?"

"There are videos, Kiara."

"Videos of what?"

"You!" I reel back in shock and shake my head.

"No, Bishop told me he lied and never recorded us." Gage's face contorts in confusion.

"What, I'm not talking about Bishop."

"Gage, you're confusing the shit out of me. What the fuck are you trying to say?" My patience is wearing thin now.

"There are videos of you and... Tony Murdoch." I reel back so fast I nearly fall from the bench. He reaches out with his good hand to stop me from falling. My breaths are coming in fast pants and my head begins to spin as I start to feel sick. He videoed what he did to me? I slump forward and rest my head between my legs trying to breathe through the nausea I'm feeling. Gage rubs my back but it does nothing to ease the disgust inside me. "I'm so sorry, doll." I can't answer him, I feel so sick knowing that others may have seen these. Oh my God. I sit up and stare at Gage in horror.

"Have you seen them?" He drops his gaze, tears sting my eyes and I can't stop them from falling.

"I only saw the first few seconds and when I saw it was you... I stopped." Bile rises up my throat, my vision becomes hazy from all the tears spilling from my eyes. I need to get the hell out of here. I stand but my legs give out. Gage catches and swings me into his arms bride style. I bury my face in his chest as I try to shut everything out, block out the world around me. I don't care where he takes me, I just need to be away from all these prying eyes. Gage knows all the details of what Tony did to me as child. He knows how he raped me and used my body for his own pleasure. He paid my mother so he could fuck me whenever he wanted. I told her what he was doing to me and all she would say was *you must have a good pussy for what he's paying me*. It had taken me months to build the courage to even tell her what was happening, as I thought she would lose her job as his maid. She was never his fucking maid. She acted like she worked there so it wouldn't raise suspicion as to why I was there all the time with the other staff and the Murdoch children.

I hear a door slam closed but still don't lift my head from his chest. I can't even dare to look at him. Me telling him about what happened is one thing but him actually seeing it with his own eyes is a whole different thing. I feel disgusted within myself daily knowing that it happened to me. I was a mere fucking child and Tony used that against me.

"I got you, doll, we're in your room. You can let it all out, I'm right here." I do, I grab at him and clutch his shirt in my hand as sobs wrack my body. I thought I was passed all of this. Yes, I do have triggers like Bishop pinning me down or being hugged from behind. I guess you never really get over trauma. Some nights I have nightmares and wake in a cold sweat when I relive the worst moments of my life even in sleep.

"What the fuck are you doing?"

"You weren't here, asshole." I wake to the sound of raised voices. I keep still when I realize it's Gage and Bishop.

"You fucking told her about the videos, didn't you?" My stomach drops, Bishop knew about them as well. Shame washes over me at the thought of him seeing what his father did to me.

"She had a fucking right to know. You can't keep this shit from her, Bishop."

"Don't tell me what I can and can't fucking do with her!"

"Yes, I can!"

"You're pushing me, Gage"

"What're you going to do, shoot me?"

"I fucking should!"

"You won't because even the great Bishop Murdoch couldn't kill his own bastard brother." *Holy shit!* Gage is related to Bishop! Oh my God, what the fuck is wrong with me? I slept with Bishop's brother and I didn't even fucking know. No wonder he was so angry when he found out.

"She's my best friend, Bish, I won't leave her. You can break my other hand if you want to but I'll always come back for her." I hear Bishop sigh behind me. I'm still tucked against Gage's chest and I have no desire to turn around and face Bishop. I don't want to see the disgust in his eyes. I didn't even fucking know that sick fuck recorded what he did to me. I feel sick all over again thinking about Bishop watching it.

"Your best friend that you're in love with, you mean?" I

feel Gage tense beneath me. I stop breathing for a minute as I wait for him to deny Bishop's claim.

"What do you want me to say. You knew from the moment you found her with me how I felt."

"But you slept with her anyway, even though I told *you* who she was to me!" I fight the flinch that flows through my body at the bitterness in Bishop's tone.

"She needed me, Bishop. She needed to know she wasn't broken or damaged. You didn't fucking see her! She broke, Bish. She fucking broke apart right in front of me and I couldn't stand the look in her eyes after she told me what happened. I would do it again and again, even if it meant I ended up here with her... loving you." My heart breaks inside my chest. I had no idea Gage felt this way about me. After we slept together, I told him that I loved him but not in that way and he said he felt the same. I feel like such a bitch for not seeing how he felt sooner. I should have known he was lying but I was too caught up with getting the fuck out of this place and running to Alaska to even notice I broke my best friend's heart.

"She's mine, Gage. I'll never let her go again." I remain still as Gage strokes my hair. I make sure to keep my eyes closed and still so he doesn't know I'm awake. I hear Bishop growl behind us, not liking the way Gage is touching me.

"She's loved you for years. She never outright said it but every time she spoke of the twins or Car, she would always mention you and how safe you made her feel. I wanted to tell her so many times that you were watching over her, even the day she got the news about her scholarship." Gage chuckles. "I don't know how someone so smart thought that they didn't have to apply for a scholarship and then suddenly one shows up for them. I wanted to tell her that she didn't have to worry about the costs of the dorms. She worried for weeks until you sent the other letter. She doesn't come from a life like you or the others. She fought tooth and fucking nail to get away from the life her mother wanted for her."

"Then why the fuck did you teach her to fight?"

"Because she needed to know how to defend herself. She was always scared of her own fucking shadow and it pissed me off, so I told her if she was to stay with me, she had to learn to fight or find somewhere else to stay."

"Why did you put her up to fight at the shack? You fucking know all the families go there to bet and meet. They could have recognized her... taken her to use against me." What the fuck, why would other mafia families know about me?

"I kept her face hidden behind face paint and I stayed with her the whole time. They would never have gotten a chance to get near her, Bishop. I would have killed them all if they tried. They may know her by name as your fiancée, but they don't know her by face." Oh my God, Bishop wasn't lying. I was promised to him years ago and I had no fucking idea. Now, some of the things Tony would say to me made sense.

I'll ruin you for that boy.

Why does he get the good pussy.

I'll wreck you before my son even gets to taste you.

A shudder rolls through me and I know Gage felt it, no point in faking anymore. I slowly blink my eyes open and cringe when I feel how puffy and crusty they are from all my tears. I have no idea how long I was out but Gage kept his word, he stayed with me the whole time and held me.

"Hey, doll." I smile up at him. "There is a really ugly guy standing behind you." Leave it to Gage to make me laugh even though I feel like shit. I hear Bishop step forward but I cling to Gage tighter. He eyes me for a beat before looking to Bishop and shaking his head. I hear him sigh behind me and I hate that I hurt him but I just can't face him right now. Not after knowing he saw me at my weakest point in my life. I know it wasn't my fault and I was just a child but never the less, shame still swells inside me.

Chapter Nineteen

Bishop

I sit on the edge of Car's bed and watch as she clings to my brother. I'm slowly coming to terms with the fact that Tony had another son that we didn't even know about until I found Kiara. Out of all the places in New York she could have wound up, she just so happened upon our father's bastard son. I've known about Gage for years but never had a reason to meet him. Tony told me he just ran the fight club and that was it. I needed to know more about the guy and where he came from, so I punched him in the face and used the blood from that to run a sample. Low and behold, I have another brother. Gage continues to stroke her hair and it takes everything inside me not to rip her off him and break his fucking nose for touching my girl.

"You gonna keep hiding all night or you gonna come

out?" She shakes her head causing Gage to chuckle. "I'll make you a deal, you come out and put your big girl panties on—" I snarl at the fucker but he ignores me. "And face my brother." I glower at him for telling her that before I could. "Yeah, I know you were awake the whole time and heard every word, you little shit." She burrows against him and hides her face in shame—I hate that Gage knows her so well. "You face him and when my hand is healed, I'll go three rounds with you." She scrambles out of his hold and rests back on her haunches, rubs her eyes and pushes her hair out of her face as she stares at him.

"You have to swear not to pull your punches." I glare at the fucker and grind my teeth. If he thinks he is laying a single finger on her I'll break both his fucking hands.

"Deal, let's make it interesting though."

"Okay?"

"Loser of each round has to lose a piece of clothing." That's it, I'm on my feet and snatching her off the bed and placing her beside me on Carlina's whilst Gage throws his head back and laughs. I sneer down at her when she joins him and laughs at my expense.

"Get the fuck out." Her laughter dies off and she tenses beside me. Gage clamps his mouth closed and looks straight at her. She gives him a small subtle shake of her head and I just know he is going to fight me on this. "Kiara?" She closes her eyes and turns her face away from me. Gage sighs and climbs to his feet, she snaps her eyes open and shoots him a pleading look. He reaches out and clasps her hand in his, giving it a gentle squeeze. He places a kiss to her forehead and I want to break his teeth for that move.

"As soon as you fell asleep, I called him. He dropped everything and came here to you when I told you you needed him, doll. Let him explain his reasons for why he didn't tell you. He's an overbearing ass but you know I wouldn't walk out of here if I thought he would hurt you." My eyes widen, my respect for him has grown. I thought I would have to throw him out of here.

"I-I... Gage."

"Shhhh, you have nothing to be scared of. Let him explain, doll." He cuts his gaze to me as he speaks again. I see the warning in his eyes. "He will not push you to speak about what happened with Tony." I nod stiffly, I've seen what happened but I don't know if I have the strength to hear her recount the events that she lived through. I couldn't even watch the full video, after a few seconds I emptied the contents of my stomach in the trash. I thought I had destroyed all the copies of those fucking things, until today. She scoots forward and shocks Gage when she wraps her arms around him and holds on, he deflates in her hold and returns her embrace.

"Thank you," she whispers.

"Just because you're with him doesn't mean I won't always be here for you. I love you, doll." I watch her melt against him and avert my gaze, I can't stand to see her touch another man like that.

"Love you to, G." Hearing those words out of her mouth is like a spear went through my fucking chest! Gage pulls back and heads out of the room. She climbs to her feet slowly and I wait to see what she is going to do. Her face is covered in tear stains and her eyes are all red and puffy from crying. "Can... I need a shower and then... we can talk." She still won't meet my gaze and it pisses me off. She turns on her heel and heads for the bathroom. Sitting here waiting for her to finish is fucking agonizing, so I pull my phone out and hit dial on Luka's number.

"Boss?"

"Have you found him?"

"I'm rerouting the IP address and trying to pin its location now. I'll try break it down for you, but he has a blocker in place that makes it so he is sending it from fifty different locations. I'm running it through my program now to pin point his exact location."

"Keep me posted. I want to know the second you find out." I end the call and dial King next.

"Bish?"

"You got the men ready to dispatch?"

"Yeap, we're all locked, loaded and ready to roll out as soon as Luka lets us know where to go."

"I would like him alive."

"If I can't make that happen?"

"Make it fucking painful then. I want the cunt to suffer for what he has done."

"You're not coming?" I sigh. Normally I always ride out with my brother when things like this happen.

"I can't leave her. Gage told her about the videos and he might come after her. The IP address could be a set up—"

"I get it, Bish."

"King?"

"Yeah."

"I'm sorry for making you leave Christine. I was wrong brother." A beat of silence passes before he finally answers.

"Bygones and all that shit. Keep your girl safe and I'll see you when this is over, B."

"Bring our sister home." I disconnect the call just as she walks in her towel and heads to her drawers. She pulls out a pair of black panties and a shirt. She drops the towel and just the sight of her naked and still dripping with droplets of water has my cock getting hard. She slips the panties on and then slips the shirt over her head.

"I know for a fucking fact that isn't my shirt!" She finally meets my gaze and I narrow my eyes when I see she is walling her emotions off from me.

"It's one of Gage's old shirts that I stole." She nibbles on her bottom lip nervously. I want to tear the fucking thing from her body and burn it. She moves toward her bed and hops up tucking her legs under herself, grabbing a pink cushion that I know my sister must have brought and holds it against her chest—almost like it's a buffer between her and I.

"You okay?" She deflates at my question.

"I don't know." She drops her head down and her hair falls forward acting like a curtain blocking her from my view. I want to reach out and push it away but I remain where I am.

"I'll explain everything about the videos if you'll answer one question."

"Okay."

"Why the fuck won't you look at me?" I can hear the bitterness in my own voice but I'm well past caring. I sat here and watched her cling to Gage and said nothing, she sits in front of me wearing his shirt and I've said nothing.

"I don't want to see the disgust in your eyes when you look at me," her whispered words break something inside me. I'm off the bed and diving across to her within a second. I nestle my way between her legs and loom over top of her. She stares up at me with tears in her eyes, her bottom lip beginning to tremble as the first tear falls. I bend down and kiss it away. She whimpers beneath me and it breaks my fucking heart. I kiss away the tears that continue to fall from her eyes. "Stop." Her quiet plea has me pulling back and resting my arms either side of her head. I search her gaze but all I see is pain.

"Talk to me."

"I didn't know there were tapes." I grit my teeth to tamper my fucking rage.

"How could you? You were a fucking kid, Kiara." She shakes her head as more tears fall.

"You saw them?"

"I erased them."

"How did Gage see it?" I won't lie to her, she deserves to know the truth.

"Tony taped what was happening and sent them to your father. He did that to you not only because he was a sick twisted bastard, but to punish your father each time he stepped out of line and tried to come for you. One of the videos was sent today—to me, King, Gage, Rook and Knight." She whimpers and I want nothing more than to take away her pain. Her eyes shine with shame.

"D-did... they see it?" I lean back on my haunches and nod solemnly. "Oh God." She shuffles up the bed until she rests against the headboard, draws her legs up and wraps her arms around them.

"They all deleted it. Luka is trying to track the IP address that sent it now. King and my men are on standby waiting for the location so they can end this and get Carlina back."

"If he tried to get me back, why would he send that video? Why would he do that to me?" I rub a hand down my face and spill the truth.

"Because... he knows I'm in love with you and knew seeing that would fuck me up." Her eyes widen and her mouth drops open in shock. I smile trying to reassure her.

"You love me?" I hold her gaze as I lay it all out for her.

"I've loved you since you were fifteen. I had no right to love a fucking child but I did anyway. I think I always did but wasn't sure until you fled. I lost it when you left, Kiara. I killed Tony, took over the role as Don and nearly destroyed our relationships with the other families searching for you. You calm the beast inside me, without you I do dumb shit. When I... kicked you out, I shot Pauly Ramano because we got a hit he was with Car. He wasn't, but killing him quieted the rage inside me for a small moment." She remains silent for a long while and I start to worry that telling her how I feel for her was the wrong move.

"How could you love me after seeing... what he did to me." I reach and grip her face between my hands and pull her up until we are eye level.

"I saw those tapes a few weeks after you ran from us. It has never changed how I feel toward you, baby, and it never fucking will. I love you, Kiara, and I don't just want to marry because of our families. I want to marry you because you make me whole and I want to be with you every second of every fucking day!" Tears flow freely down her cheeks and I groan internally, why the fuck do I keep making her cry? She pushes my arms away and wraps her arms around my neck, pulling me to her so she can kiss me. I can feel everything she hasn't said in this kiss. Before I can deepen the kiss, she pulls back and rests her head against mine.

"I've loved you since I was nine years old. I think I always have, even after I ran from Tony." Pride swells inside me at her whispered declaration. I kiss her again and haul her against me so I can hold her close. Even after everything my father did to her, she can still be here with me and love me. Kiara Bennett is the strongest fucking woman I know and I'll spend the rest of my life trying to make up for all the wrongs that have happened to her in her life.

Chapter Twenty

Kiara

The sound of a phone ringing stirs me awake. I feel Bishop stir behind me and smile. He made love to me, slow sweet passionate love for the first time and fucking hell, Bishop fucking me rough is hot but Bishop taking his time and showing me how much he loves me through his body had me screaming so fucking loud that I hoped all the cheer bitches could hear. Bishop flicks on the bed side lamp and grabs his phone. He checks the caller I.D before hitting the green button.

"Yeah?" Whatever Bishop hears on the other end of the phone has him throwing the covers off and jumping to his feet. I sit up in a panic. "How long?" He grabs his pants and starts to get dressed. "Keep me updated, we're leaving now."

He drops his phone to the bed before turning to me. "Get dressed."

"What, why?"

"Now, Kiara, we have to go." I climb off the bed to do as he asks, the panic in his voice tells me something bad happened or is about to. As I'm pulling on a pair of jeans, he grabs his phone and calls someone. "Get the twins and Mav and meet me at my car." He hangs up and puts his phone in his pocket. I grab my Chucks and slip in my feet in them. As soon as I stand, he grabs my hand and hauls me from the room, he's moving so fast I can't keep up with his long strides.

"Bishop, slow down!" He doesn't, instead he turns and lifts me in his arms. I cling to him like a monkey and lock my legs around his waist as he heads for the stairwell. He takes the stairs two at a time and I close my eyes in fear, if he slips I'm going to be squished beneath his weight! When he reaches the bottom floor, he kicks the door open and runs through the foyer. I peer over my shoulder and see it's still dark out, it must be early hours of the morning now. He kicks open the outside door, races down the stairs of the dorm building and heads for the carpark. "What's going on?" I ask, my adrenaline is finally giving way to panic now that we are outside in the middle of the fucking night running away from something. I spot four figures running toward us from the boy's dorms and tense, until they pass by a lantern and I see Mav, Gage and the twins hurrying toward us. Bishop stops, then places me on my feet next to his car. He spins around and waits for the others.

"What's going on?" Knight demands. Bishop reaches into his pocket and pulls out a key that he hands to Knight.

"You and Rook take Kiara and go to the safe house."

"What the fuck?"

"Shut the fuck up, Knight, do as I say and go now!" Knight rushes around to the driver side and pops the lock. Rook stands beside Bishop and waits. "What?"

"Anthony is here, isn't he?" Bishop reaches out and lays a hand on his baby brother's shoulder—Rook is a few inches shorter than Bishop.

"Take Knight and Kiara and go, brother. I'll catch up to you soon." Rook nods as Bishop turns to face me, the look of regret in his eyes has me wanting to hold him close and ease his worries but I know right now, he needs to be the Mafia boss and not my lover. He reaches out, grips my face, then kisses me. I feel all his love and devotion in this kiss. I cling to his jacket wanting to keep him here with me. He breaks the kiss and pulls back stepping out of my hold, turns his back to me without a glance and heads back toward the school with Mav following after him. Gage comes to me and rests his hands atop my shoulders, trying to smile reassuringly.

"Go with the twins and let him focus on ending this. Once this is done you can live out your fantasies or whatever that is."

"Gage?"

"Hmm?"

"Don't let him die... I can't—" He cuts me off by pulling me to him and hugging me.

"I'll bring him back to you, doll. I promise." With that said, he places a quick kiss to the top of my head and turns, chasing after Bishop and Mav. Rook clears his throat and holds the door open for me to climb in. I do as he says and buckle myself in as Knight starts the car. Once Rook is inside, Knight peels out of the car park so fast, I sling back against the seat. The tension in the car is high. I know both of them are worried about their brother, I just hope King

143

and the others can get here in time to help. I don't know if my... father is alone or not, I don't know the guy yet a pang of regret shoots through me at the thought of him dying by the hands of the man I love. I may not know him but hearing that he tried to come for me and has an actual good reason why he didn't, has me softening toward him.

Dawn is breaking by the time we pull into a driveaway of a secluded cabin. I dozed on and off most of the way, not taking in where we were going. I don't need to know, the fact that Bishop knows where I am settles me. All I care about is him coming back to me unharmed, we can sort everything else out later. I know I sound like a selfish bitch for worrying about myself and not Carlina—I mean I am worried about her and how she is and if she is okay—but I'm more worried about her brother. I don't care if that makes me the worst friend ever, but I love Bishop and I fucking deserve to have him. After everything we both have gone through in our lives, we should get to have what we want.

"Come on, princess." I follow the twins out of the car. Rook wraps an arm around my shoulders and pulls me into his side as we approach a log cabin. I shiver when a cold breeze strikes. "Welcome to the cold. New England is a bitch in winter so be thankful it isn't here yet." We're in New England? Fuck, how long were we driving for? Rook ushers me through the door after Knight who flicks a couple switches and the room is bathed in light. It's exactly as you would think a cabin would look like on the inside. Animal trophies on the wall, plaid couches, open fire place, high ceilings, antler chandeliers, and I see a staircase to the left.

"Let's get some sleep." Knight's voice sounds gruff from

hours of not using it. I'm tired but I know I'll never be able to sleep until I know if Bishop is okay. I also don't want the twins staying up because of me, so I sigh and nod my head as Knight leads the way up the stairs. Rook bids us good night as he claims the first room on the right. We pass three more doors before stopping in front of the last one at the end. "This is Bishop's room. I figured he'd want you in here." I smile up at Knight, wishing I knew what caused him to change from the smiley happy kid he was to this closed off angry guy.

"Thanks, are you okay?" He sighs and runs a hand through his brown hair.

"I will be, get some sleep," is all he says before he turns and claims the second room on the right. I open the door and flick the light on. Bishop's room has massive bay windows on one side, his own bathroom and closet... of course it's fucking neat and tidy. A big king bed decorated in black sheets and pillows sits in the middle. I'm too tired to even look around and be nosey. I crawl on the bed and rest back against the pillows, before I know it I'm drifting off to sleep with Bishop being the last thought in my mind.

The sound of an alarm blaring through the house has me sitting up in bed in fright. The door flings open and I scream, until I see a shirtless Rook standing there with fear etched all over his face.

"What happened?" I demand.

"We have to go, now!" I leap from the bed like it's on fire and race toward Rook. He grips my hand in his and we race down the hall, then down the stairs. Knight burst through the front door, slamming it closed and locking it.

Beside the door he enters a code in the keypad and the alarm shuts off. The ringing in my ears continues for a few more seconds until I spot a gun in Knight's hand, I turn to Rook and spot one in his free hand as well. Dread pools inside me. They exchange a look and I know they are doing their weird twin communication thing.

"Take her to the basement and keep her down there." I try to yank free of his hold but Rook holds firm, nods to Knight, then he's dragging me through the cabin past the living room and into the kitchen, where he rips open the door to the pantry and puts a code in on the side of the wall. The back wall opens revealing a staircase. I fight hard to get free but he yanks me forward and pulls me down the stairs after him. The lights in here must be motion activated as they turn on as we pass. I stub my toe on the bottom step and curse but Rook doesn't pay me any mind as he drags me into a room and pushes me inside. I stumble a couple steps before whirling around to face him, ready to fight my way out of here if I have to.

"Stay here, Kiara!" He attempts to close the door but I dart forward and grip it topping him.

"What the fuck is going on?"

"He followed us, your father is here and Bishop and the others are fucking hours away so I need you to stay here so Knight and I can handle this."

"I can help." I try to reason with him, I won't just stay in a fucking room while they risk their lives.

"You can't and Bishop would kill us if anything happened to you."

"Rook, please." He pulls out his phone and chucks it to me, I release the door to catch it.

"He has men surrounding the fucking place and my sister on her knees out front with a gun to her fucking head, stay here Kiara and shut up!" I don't fight him when he yanks the door closed. I stare at it for a moment stunned silent as I think about the fear that must be coursing through Carlina at the moment. I turn away from the door and take in my surroundings. A single bed on one side and a chair on the other, that's it. I grip my hair and tug on the strands. He set Bishop up knowing he would send me away to keep me safe. He fucking knew Bishop would send all his men to the school, which left me, Rook and Knight defenseless. The sound of Rook's phone ringing has me nearly jumping out of my skin. When I see Bishop's name flashing, I hit the button.

"Bishop?" A relieved sigh comes from him before he speaks.

"I'm coming, baby. Stay in the basement with the twins—"

"They aren't with me," I cut in. Bishop curses on the other end of the phone and shouts at someone to drive faster.

"Where are they?" I can hear the anger in his tone and know it isn't directed at me. He's worried for his brothers and their safety.

"Knight's upstairs and Rook just brought me down here and told me to stay put," I whisper.

"Fuck!" I hear him punching something and cringe. "Stay there, baby. I'm on my way." Tears cloud my vision as realization dawns on me, I know what I have to do.

"I love you, Bishop."

"Kiara, don't you fucking dare go out there!" he roars, the pain in his voice almost makes me listen to his command.

"I won't let your brothers or your sister die for me." He tries to cut in but I push on needing to get this out before I lose my nerve. "I've loved you most of my life and I'll love you in the next one as well. Goodbye, my love." I ignore his pleas as I end the call and chuck it on the bed. It rings again but I ignore it as I open the door and ready myself to meet my father and end this.

I creep silently through the house, not wanting to risk making a noise and alerting the twins that I'm up here. I peer around the corner of the kitchen and when I see the front door open and hear their voices from outside my heart sinks. I race toward the door and hide to the side as I listen in on what they are saying.

"Let her go!" Knight sounds vicious, the sound of his cold tone has me standing tall and proud.

"Give me my daughter and your sister goes free." I still at the sound of his voice, it's melodic and sure.

"She isn't here, we don't know where she is." I love Rook for wanting to keep me safe but he shouldn't have to. I take a deep breath and steel my spine as I twirl around and stand in the open doorway with my hands raised above my head.

"I'm here." Rook and Knight both turn to me, fear and anger swirls in the depths of both their eyes. I shrug my shoulders. "I can't let you guys do this." I look beyond them and that's when I spot Car on her knees with her head down and a gun pressed to the back of it. I follow his arm up and when I land on his face my breath hitches. "Mr. Rogers?" He smirks at me. I never took notice of my history teacher until now—he doesn't wear his normal glasses and his hair isn't a mess like I'm used to. His black hair is slicked back against his head, his pale blue eyes bore into mine—his aren't as pale as mine though. He smiles wide and I watch as some of the tension bleeds out of him. He wears a suit like Bishop but doesn't fill it out the way B does. Bishop wears the suit but my father's suit seems like it wears him. He doesn't seem comfortable in it, almost like he never wears them unless he has to.

"Hello, Kiara." I slowly lower my hands to my sides and step forward until I stand in the middle of the twins. I look down at Carlina and cock my head to the side, her hair blocks her face from us. Her camisole shirt is loose and stained, she wears...leggings. I dart my gaze to my father's in shock.

"That's not Carlina." I feel the twin gaze on me but don't dare look away from the man in front of me. A smile spreads wide across his face. He lowers his gun and tucks it into his holster inside his jacket. I look around and that's when I see all the men with their guns all trained on the twins and me by default for standing between them. The woman slowly stands and dusts off her pants before flicking her hair from her face, it's not Car. The woman doesn't say a word as she turns and heads toward one of the cars behind Anthony and his men. Rook steps forward with his gun raised, I hear all the guns around cocking and ready to shoot.

"Where is my sister?" His relaxed expression switches to hatred in a matter of seconds as he stares at Rook.

"I would never hold a gun to my daughter-in-law's head like that." I gasp, Rook sways slightly and Knight remains stoic and still as he stares at Anthony.

"What?" I ask, he looks to me and smiles wide.

"Oh, my dear, the sweet Carlina is now your sister. Isn't that wonderful?" I don't know if he's joking or if he's actually being serious. There is no way I can have a brother. Bishop told me I'm the only heir to the Bennett family.

"What the fuck did you do to my sister?" I can hear the worry in Rook's voice and I want to reach out and comfort him, but I don't.

"Would you like to meet your brother?" I just stare at him too shocked to even utter a word. He raises his hand in the air and I hear a car door open. We wait with bated breath as two figures head toward us. It's still too dark out to see them clearly. When they step up beside Anthony, my mouth drops open and my eyes widen.

"What the fuck are you doing here?" Knight snaps. I'm unable to form words as I stare at him, unable to process the fact that he of all people is my brother!

Chapter Twenty-One

Bishop

So many different scenarios are running through my mind about what could be happening. Gage drives like a mad man but we are still over an hour away. I can't get a hold of the twins and my gut is churning at the thought of something happening to them. I know my brothers would risk their lives for Kiara because of what she means to me. I've never felt so fucking helpless in my life. I know Gage is driving as fast as he can without killing us but it still isn't quick enough. I should have never sent the three of them away, I should have kept them with me where they would be safe and I would be able to protect her and my little brothers.

"Fuck!" I roar as I punch the dash of the Range Rover for the sixth time in the past hour.

"We'll get there, Bish—"

"What if we're too fucking late, King?"

"We won't be. The boys are smart and know how to protect themselves, and Kiara isn't a rookie either."

"Damn right she isn't!" Gage chimes in. I lull my head to the side and stare at him. Even after everything I have done to him, he's still here helping us. I vow silently to myself to treat him better from this moment on, starting with moving him into the family home and making him one of us.

"How many fights did she lose at the shack?" A proud smile crosses his face.

"None, she is the undefeated woman's champ." I hear King whistle behind me. Mav and Luka clap like idiots, pride swells inside me. My girl is a badass and I guess I owe that to Gage for training her. Instead of being a pussy and watching from afar, he took charge and taught her how to defend herself in case a situation like she is in now arose.

Gage stops the car down the road and kills the engine, the cars behind do the same. I want to go in guns blazing but I also know that approach would likely get them killed. We slip out of the cars and close the doors quietly. I pull my gun and check the mag making sure I'm full. Gage hands me another two mags and I nod my thanks. King comes around the back and chucks a bullet proof vest at me.

"Put the fucking thing on and don't be a tough fuck. Not even you can stop a bullet," he snaps quietly. I do as he says and strap the vest on, I instruct my guys to spread out around the property but make sure to stay hidden until I give the order. Luka and Mav follow after them while Gage,

King and I go to the front. We jog till we reach the end of the drive and I can hear voices in the distance. I hear a man and he sounds panicked, I look to King who shrugs his shoulders as we slowly creep up the drive. We duck behind a tree and see all the cars and men scattered around, there is no way we are getting inside to them.

"I need you both to cover me," I whisper. Gage grabs the front of my vest and yanks me to him getting right in my face.

"Don't be a stupid prick, they will shoot you on sight—" Gage is cut off by the sound of Knight's shout.

"You fucking give me my sister or I put a bullet between her fucking eyes!" Everything inside me freezes. Gage drops his hold on me, I see it in his eyes he knows exactly who Knight is talking about as well. King has a horrified look on his face, but before he can reach for me I turn and run. I hear him and Gage behind me. I draw my gun and fire at the fucker who turns around. Gage and King fire off shots as well. They scatter back and duck behind the cars for coverage but I don't care, I need to get to Knight before he does something he can't come back from. He won't survive going through something like this, not after last time.

"Stop fucking shooting!" I stop running when they all come into view. Rook faces Knight who has Kiara on her knees facing him. I spot Carlina out of the corner of my eye standing next a man who I assume is Anthony Bennett. I glare at the boy beside my sister when I recognize him.

"You," I growl out, the punk smirks at me and flicks his brows.

"Me," the smart fucker replies. King brushes past me and raises his hands as Knight looks to him.

"Put the gun down, brother, you don't want to hurt Kiara." The look in Knight's eyes tells me he has gone inside his own head, our Knight is no longer in control. I tuck my gun into my waistband and unstrap my vest dropping it on the ground as I move toward my brother. I eye Anthony out of the corner of my eye, he tries to remain calm and collected at the situation but I can see the sweat that beads his brow. He's shitting himself at the possibility of Knight killing Kiara as much as me. I push my pride and ego aside as I face him, he pulls his gaze from Knight to look at me.

"Pull your men back." He scoffs.

"So you can kill me in cold blood? I don't think so." I grit my teeth in anger ready to tear him a new one until Carlina steps forward, her brown eyes hold no anger in them. She should be furious with me for not finding her sooner. She turns her back to me and faces the assholes.

"My brother won't hurt either of you."

"How can you be so sure?" I knew I should have gone after this punk-ass fucking kid myself for touching my girl.

"Because he wouldn't want to hurt me like that, Quinn."

"The fuck I wouldn't," I snap. Car turns and peers over her shoulder at me, I can see the cunning look she shoots me and I nod. "I swear I won't harm them."

"Give me your gun, it will put them at ease." I pull my gun from my waistband letting Carlina know with a single look that she better know what she is doing. Anthony commands his men to fall back as I approach Knight with my hands raised. I stop a couple feet away when he cuts a glance at me. Rook moves to stand shoulder to shoulder beside me.

"You can put it away, brother. No one needs to get hurt." Rook tries to appeal to his twin but Knight is too far inside his own mind to hear him. I close my eyes and pluck up the courage to voice my little brother's secret.

"She isn't her, Knight. Kiara didn't hurt you." I can feel King and Rook's stares boring into me, I'm the only one who knows Knight's deepest darkest secret. Because I protected one brother while my other one pulled away from me and blames me for his struggles daily.

"She should have fucking died!" Kiara doesn't flinch when he pushes the gun against her forehead.

"She did, Knight, she's dead." I don't know how the bitch died but I'm glad she is dead. I don't know who killed her but if I find them, I'll thank them myself.

"I'm so sorry," Kiara whispers up to me. I need her to shut up or risk her pissing him off further. "Whatever happened, Knight, I'll help you. I'll be here for you and help you through whatever trauma you have. I'm not perfect, no one is, but the scars of our past don't define us. We are not victims, we're survivors." Whatever she is saying seems to be getting through to him. His eyes seem to focus more and when he looks down at her again a horrified look overtakes his features. He drops his gun and stumbles back a step. Relief flows through me. I step forward to grab Kiara but a shot rings out. I dart my gaze to Knight and watch as he clutches his chest as blood soaks through his shirt. I spin around with my heart in my throat. Quinn still has his gun in the air with a proud smile on his face while Anthony stares at him in horror. Carlina spins toward him, lifts my gun and aims it at the side of his head as she pulls the trigger. She doesn't even flinch as he falls, a twisted smile graces her beautiful face. Gage reaches her but he's too late as he tackles her to the ground. King rushes past me and I turn back to Knight, his head resting in Rook's lap. Kiara is kneeling at his side holding her hands on the wound to staunch the flow of blood.

"Call 911!" Rook shouts. I stand here frozen in place as

I stare down at my brothers and Kiara. Rook has tears flowing down his cheeks as he cradles his twins head in his lap, Kiara keeps telling him to keep his eyes open and stay with us. I've never frozen before in my life, even when I had gun in my face, but the sight of my brother laying there bleeding out and there isn't a fucking thing I can do about it has me frozen in place. I don't know what the fuck to do. King lifts Knight from Rook's lap and ignores Kiara and Rook's cries to stop. He spins around and the look he shoots me has me shaking out of my stunned state.

"Get your fucking head in the game, deal with Anthony, I'll deal with Knight." I nod my head as he rushes past me. Rook is hot on his heels as he races after King. Gage chucks Rook the car keys as he runs past. Carlina is on her feet staring down at Quinn's body smiling. Kiara moves past me and goes to my sister. She stands in front of her and gently reaches for her hands. Car blinks a few times before finally looking at Kiara, her eyes are void of all emotion.

Chapter Twenty-Two

Kiara

Her eyes look hollow, her hands are cold to the touch. She doesn't look innocent and free anymore, she seems more mature and... tortured. What the fuck happened to her? Gage slides up beside her and gives me a nod, letting me know he has her while I deal with Bishop and Anthony. I look around as the sun slowly begins to rise and darkness fades. I see Anthony's men facing away from us with their guns drawn and pointed at Bishop's men. I spot Mav and Luka and pray they don't get shot. I focus on Anthony and find his gaze already on me, the awe in his gaze shocks me.

"I don't want anyone else to get hurt," I plead. Anthony searches my gaze for a tense moment before he speaks.

"I'll let them all go if you agree to come with me." I open my mouth to deny him but when I feel the wall of muscle at my back I relax slightly and know he's back to himself. Seeing Knight go down clearly caused him to clam up.

"She isn't going anywhere with you!" Anthony glances at Bishop briefly before focusing back on me.

"The choice is yours, Kiara." Bishop grips my waist and pulls me back so I'm flush against his front. I look down at Quinn's body and fight the bile that wants to come out of me. His eyes are open and staring lifelessly ahead, I quickly avert my gaze and look to Anthony.

"How was he my brother?" Anthony sighs and runs a hand through his hair, for someone who lost a son he doesn't seem very distraught.

"He wasn't by blood. He was my deceased wife's son. He wasn't very bright and he sure as hell didn't have what it takes to lead this family." His careless words stun me for a beat. I didn't know Quinn long, I thought he was a good guy and a great friend up until he shot Knight. As soon as he pulled that trigger, he became enemy number one! "Pull your men back."

"Get fucked." Anthony's gaze hardens as he looks to Bishop.

"I'll kill you and all your men while she watches. Your family will be nothing by the time I'm finished with you!" The conviction in his tone tells me he isn't bullshitting.

"You hurt him, you hurt me!" I interject. Anthony looks thoroughly confused by my declaration.

"You don't have to be afraid of them anymore, I know it took me a long time but I'm here, Kiara. He and his family can't hurt you anymore. I swear to you that you will be safe with me." I scoff.

"That worked out real fucking well for Quinn, didn't it?"

"Quinn made his choice when he chose to pull that trigger!"

"What about Car. Did she make the choice to marry Quinn?" Anthony rolls his eyes skyward, like he is running out of patience with me.

"She never married him, it's called stacking my chips. I had to show you all I had the upper hand and by my count, I still do. We out number you three to one."

"Bullshit, I have more men here than you do," Bishop snaps.

"You stupid fool, you know nothing. You see a few of my men here in front of your lackeys but what you don't see are my other behind yours. You're cornered, I believe the term is...checkmate?" I cringe at the play on Bishop and his brother's names. Anthony could be full of shit but what if he isn't and we really are cornered? I can't risk them getting hurt.

"What do you want?" I ask.

"For you to come home where you always should have been."

"You fucked a whore and got her pregnant, surely you can find someone better to marry and make more babies?" His face contorts in confusion.

"What makes you think your mother was a whore?"

"She sold herself for a hit and sold... me." Anger blazes in his blue eyes.

"She wasn't a whore, she was my wife, then she ran with you because we had a fucking spat. Tony offered her a safe haven and then got her hooked on drugs." I slam back into Bishop, floored at Anthony's declaration.

"She was your wife?"

"We had been promised to each other since we were twelve." I shake my head unable to accept what he is saying.

159

"I speak the truth, Kiara. Come with me and I'll tell you everything." Bishop's hold on me tightens and I love him for not butting in and taking control of the situation like he wants to.

"I won't leave, any of them." I'm proud of myself when my voice doesn't waiver. He looks between Bishop and I, his gaze calculating and suspicious.

"You care for them?"

"Yes," I say with a hundred percent conviction.

"Even after what they did?" I scowl at him when I feel Bishop tense behind me.

"*They* didn't do anything to me. Their piece of shit father hurt me, not them. Bishop and the others aren't monsters like their sperm donor. You want me to come with you, fine. But just know I'll never stop trying to escape you. I'll fight you every single day until I get free to come back to him. If any part of you as my father cares about me at all, you will walk away now and not hurt any of them." He remains silent for a while, mulling over what I just said. He reaches up and scratches the scruff on his chin. I feel like an idiot for not seeing the resemblance between us sooner. He was right in front of me this whole time, hiding in plain sight.

"How can I walk away from you, Kiara? I dedicated the last eighteen years of my life trying to find you. You were ripped away from me when you were just a baby. The only time I would get pictures of you was before your mother met Tony... five thousand dollars a picture she would charge me. Her father hid her and you from me when she fled. I destroyed her whole family and still lost you." He turns away from me and runs a hand through his hair. I can hear the anguish in his voice, it hurts me. I turn and peer up at Bishop. His gaze implores me not to but he should know by now I don't do as I'm told. I break away from him and step around Quinn's body. Anthony turns to me and I stop a foot away. The look in his eyes opens something inside me. I've never known the love of a parent, so to have him staring at me like he would burn the world to the ground in my honor stumps me. Longing springs to life inside me, something I haven't felt since I was a child. The need to be loved and held by a parent who wants me, who doesn't treat me like shit. I never had a mother that did my hair, took me for mani-pedis or even just held me when I skinned my knee. I was nothing to her except a way to pay for her habit, a tool to be used for her own gain.

"I don't know what to say to you. I want to believe everything you are saying but it's not like I have experience with what a good parent should be like. If you mean what you say, don't hurt the man that I love or the people I care about." His gaze burns. I can see he wants to deny me and take the revenge he has craved for years. I move forward and leave a foot of space between us. We stare into each other's eyes and that's when I see it, the longing. He's so fast when he reaches out and yanks me against him. I hear Bishop rush forward but stop when Anthony wraps his arms around me and buries his face against my head. I stand stiff for a moment, shocked as hell. I don't know what I'm supposed to do, but as if my body knows what to do, my arms lift of their own accord and wrap around him. He melts at my touch and all the tension flees my body. I live in this moment and embrace the thought of being loved and wanted by the father I was told hated the sight of me and wanted nothing to do with me. He pulls back and grips my face between his hands smiling down at me. I see unshed tears in his eyes.

"I wish I could give you what you want but now that I have you in my sights, I won't be able to walk away." I tense again, expecting him to turn on Bishop and the others. "I will agree to not hurt them *if* you agree to meet with me weekly." Before I can protest, he pushes on. "I only want to get to know my daughter, nothing more. Please, Kiara. I am begging you. Give me a chance to show you I am not like your mother."

"How can you say that, your step son was just killed and you didn't bat an eye but you stand here and claim to care for me?"

"Quinn was an idiot. He thinks I had no idea that he was planning to kill me and then you so he would be the one to take over *our* family. He is not a Bennett, but you are. Everything I have will be yours—."

"She won't be a Bennett for long!" Bishop's words send a shiver down my spine, I hear the conviction in his words. Anthony glances at Bishop briefly before dismissing him like he is nothing but a nuisance.

"You don't have to marry a Murdoch. I'm here now and they cannot make you do anything you don't want to do." Call me stupid but I believe him. I believe that Anthony would take Bishop and all his men out now if I was to ask, but that isn't what I want.

"He isn't making me do anything I don't want to do, now that you're here he may actually let me travel." I try to jest to lighten the mood.

"If you wanting to travel means getting away from *him*, I'll fuel the jet now and take you wherever you want." It may not be the right moment but laughter bubbles out of me, Anthony smiles and for the first time since seeing him tonight this one reaches his eyes.

"Thank you but all I want to do right now is go to the hospital and make sure Knight is okay."

Chapter Twenty-Three

Bishop

We sit in the waiting room of the hospital. Rook looks as pale as a ghost. Carlina just stares ahead at a blank wall in a world of her own. Gage and King stand in the corner of the room, while Kiara and I sit in the hard plastic chairs. I cut my gaze to the man sitting on her other side and grind my teeth. Anthony Bennett agreed to let us go but on the condition he came with us, the fucker wasn't lying. He had us outnumber and outgunned, he could have slaughtered us and taken Kiara but he didn't, he swore to her that he wouldn't do anything to upset her. Every fiber of my being wants to say he's lying and planning to do something to my family but, that is only because I never had a good role model as a parent. I agreed to him coming here if he sent his men away. The fucker agreed and came alone without a single man to watch his back. I don't know if he is cocky or if he is a man of his word and expects me to do the same.

Rook and King were pissed when they saw him. Gage and I had to hold them back before they killed him. I look out the glass window to the side and see the same Escalade drive past and smirk, Anthony cocks a brow at me.

"You didn't think I trusted you?" I narrow my eyes ready to tear the fucker a new asshole but pause when Kiara places her hand on my leg.

"Fucking pussy," I mutter as I slouch back in my chair. Mav and Luka rush through the entry and come straight for us. I told them to deal with our men and put a tail on Anthony, I won't be caught unprepared again.

"Boss?"

"What?" Luka looks to Mav before facing me again.

"The Ramano's." I'm on my feet and ushering the two of them to the other side of the room. When I'm sure we are out of hearing distance I signal for him to continue. "We just got word that they are planning a retaliation for Pauly's death." Fuck, I can't focus on this shit right now, I need to see that Knight is okay before I can focus on anything else. If the Ramano's want a fucking war they will get one!

"Tail them, report back to me. I want to know when they shit, what they eat and where they go." Mav and Luka nod before turning and leaving.

Kiara is resting her head in my lap sleeping, King has taken Rook and Car to get something to eat from the café, Gage is off doing whatever the fuck he is doing. Anthony sits opposite me just staring at her. I look down at her with my jacket draped over her sleeping form. She looks peaceful, looking at her now you wouldn't think she has faced the horrors that she has in her short life. She went through fucking hell at the hands of my father, how she come out the other side and not bitter and hating the world I will never know. She possesses a strength inside her I never will. I stroke her hair marveling at how silky the strands feel between my fingers, fatigue gnaws inside me but I'll never sleep a wink with my enemy sitting across me.

"I will never support this." I swing my gaze to him. He keeps his focus on Kiara. The way he looks at her like he has some claim on the woman I love grates on my fucking nerves. She's mine and I will never let her go.

"I don't give a fuck, she's mine and will remain with me. You try anything to take her from me and I'll bury you six feet fucking deep." A condescending smile crosses his face as looks to me.

"You are but a boy trying to play in a man's world. I have more power, more money and more men than you do. I'll wipe out your entire family and not bat an eye or lose a wink of sleep over it."

"Try it you—"

"Shut up boy and listen!" My fingers itch to reach for my gun. "You can reach for your gun. You can try to take me out but just know this, I own the fucking hospital. I own half the shares in all the other hotels and clubs you are trying to acquire. Why do you think your land deals and sales aren't going through?" I keep the shock from my face, this dirty old fucker has been building a backlist while we try to play catch up and fix all Tony's fucking mess. "You want to take me out? You need to learn how to play the long game. You and your brothers are named after chess pieces yet you play like checkers. You are still breathing right now because my daughter willed it be that way. If she changes her mind, I will not hesitate to end you and your family."

"You had my sister, why not take her out? You had the means and the opportunity to do it, if what you say is true, you never needed Car alive to get to me." His eyes glaze over for a moment as he grits his teeth.

"I do have the means. I never laid a single finger on your sister, nor did any of my men. I had planned to kill you the day you came to the school."

"Why did you take Car and why didn't you kill me?"

"Kiara's videos weren't the only ones I received." His voice is filled with loathing and disgust and it makes me sick to think of my father sending videos of my girl and his own fucking daughter! "You're alive because of how Kiara reacted toward you. If I didn't see the... love in her eyes the day you walked into my class you would be dead. I would have also killed your brothers at the cabin for standing in my way."

"Why would Tony send you videos of his own daughter, why would you care about my sister?" His eyes harden and crinkle at the corners.

"I may be a part of this life but that doesn't mean I'm like the others. I don't dabble in the sex trade, never have and never fucking will. Tony was a huge investor with the Bratva and in case you haven't noticed your holdings are losing value because the Russian's are pissed."

"So?"

"My daughter will not become collateral damage because of something your father did. The Russian's will come for you and your family for stopping their monthly shipments." Everything begins to click into place. Ever since I took over for Tony, nothing I have done has seemed to appease the other four families in New York, now I know why.

"I will never be a part of something like that. *If* they come, I will be ready."

"Not *if*, but *when*. They will come for you, boy. Either you take them out before they get here or you put your family in danger. Prove to me you're nothing like your father and actually do care for my daughter and I might be swayed to help you take out your enemies." I scoff.

"Like the other families where you come from will agree to that." He quirks a brow and smiles cockily at me.

"What other families?" My eyes widen.

"You run Florida, on your own?" He nods. "How?"

"I married her mother to make peace, when Kiara's grandfather hid her and her mother from me, I killed them. It caused an uproar with the other families. It was kill or be killed and needless to say, the streets ran red with their blood and not mine." I stay silent mulling over his words, I know he has a double meaning to them I just need to figure out what that is. Kiara sits up and pulls my focus to her, she smiles at me before turning to face her father. I can see from the look on her face that the little minx has been awake listening this whole time.

"You want Bishop to take out the other families and put his brothers as the heads so they will run New York." A proud smile stretches across his face as he nods at his daughter.

"Clever you are, my dear. If you want to stop the Russian's from coming after you and your family you need more men. You need this city locked down and ready to fight at a moment's notice."

"It will take time," I grit out as I wrap my arm around

Kiara. She huddles into my side and rests her cheek against my chest.

"You don't have time, the families are already plotting against you." I glare at the bastard.

"How would you know that?"

"How do you think I was able to roam freely through this city with an army and not have you alerted?" My hold on Kiara tightens. Those double-crossing sons of bitches sold me out because I refuse to steal little girls who haven't even bled yet and ship them off to be whores. I'll kill each and every one of those fuckers forever thinking they could cross the Murdoch family and live to tell the tale.

"As soon as Knight is out of here, it will be war." Anthony's eyes sparkle with glee. He may be calm and kind in front of his daughter but even I can see the beast beneath his mask that thirsts for the blood of his enemies. The beast inside me thirsts for the same thing.

Chapter Twenty-Four

Kiara

6 days later...

Knight is finally home. He will be off the football field for the rest of the season but he doesn't seem to be worried about that. He hasn't looked at me since we picked him up from the hospital, or spoken to any of us. Rook is taking it the hardest having his twin shut him out. Bishop has ordered Rook to return to school even though he has rebelled against the idea. Car and I are going back Monday, which means I only have the weekend with Bishop. He's agreed to let me go back without Gage or Mav because Anthony has said he will resume his position as my history teacher and will have men surrounding the whole school. I don't know what has changed between them or how they became *frenemies* but I'm not mad about it. King is pissed about it but has managed to keep his thoughts to himself. Anthony has been nothing but kind and true to his word.

He has called me daily and we even went to dinner last night, it was weird at first and I felt awkward until not two minutes after we sat down to eat, did Bishop stroll in. Anthony just laughed and said he was wondering how long it would take before he gave up tailing us and just joined. I know there is bad blood between them and I'm choosing to stay out of it. Anthony has offered to pay for a councilor if I want. I've been mulling over the idea for days now and I just don't know if that is something I can do. I don't want to relive the past but I also don't want it to hold me back either.

"Can I sit?" I close the book I wasn't even reading and look up to Car smiling and nod. She sits on the lounger next to me. I hate that her eyes are hidden behind her sunglasses, we haven't spent any time together since we've been back. It's almost like the night we were all back together was the last time we were all together. They never stay in the room with one of their siblings long enough as there is a huge divide in the house and I don't know how to help Bishop or any of them fix it. Car and I used to be so close but now I feel like I don't have the right to pry into her business. She hasn't told any of us what happened and Anthony refuses to speak on the matter until Carlina is ready. "You know, I used to love sitting out here as a girl and swimming with my brothers." She smiles fondly.

"What happened?" Her smile vanishes.

"I learned my father was a monster and I was nothing more than some hole he could sink his cock into whenever he wanted." I flinch at the harsh edge to her tone. "He wanted to break me, he thought he did at one point."

"Car, if you want to talk about what happened with... Anthony, I'm here for you."

"Why do you all assume it was bad?" That catches my attention, I stare at her utterly confused.

"Wasn't it?" I question. She lulls her head to the side and stares at me.

"Can I trust you to keep a secret?" I don't hesitate.

"Yes." She lifts her glasses and holds my stare as she adds.

"You cannot tell my brother." I gulp but nod my agreement. "We will be talking about you fucking my brother behind my back as well, you're not off the hook for that." I smile and so does she. She may act pissed but I can tell she is happy Bishop and I are together.

"I'm not coming back to school with you." I sit up in my seat and stare at her confused.

"What do you mean?"

"My brothers want me to finish school and be the good princess I should be. I don't want that life. I've never been smart like you or Knight, King has his thing with Bishop and Rook has football but I haven't found my thing yet. I need to find out who I am and I can't do that with my brothers all telling me who I *should* be."

"Car—"

"Please, Kiara, don't say a word to Bishop. If you tell him he'll stop me and I swear I will never speak to you again. I'll leave a note or whatever, I'll call you or text you every couple of days but just... make him see I need this." I reach over and grip her hand. She sits forward and I see the tears in her eyes. I may not need counseling or something like that to heal but Car needs this to help her move on from her past.

"I swear." She smiles but I add on. "You have to text

171

every second day and at least send a picture of you with a cocktail so I know you aren't being held hostage—" She cuts me off when she launches herself at me. I laugh but return her embrace and savor this moment between us. I never knew what love was until I met the Murdoch siblings, it seems only fitting that after years of feeling like I could never love again that they are the ones to make my heart beat for something other than just keeping me alive.

———

I exit the shower in my towel and pause in the entry to our bedroom, the black satin sheets are covered in rose petals, the lights are turned down to a soft glow. Vases of roses adorn the bed side tables, the dressers and the ottoman at the foot of the bed. I look around and pause when I spot a shadow lurking in the corner.

"B, what is all of this?" He steps forward and my mouth unhinges. He's shirtless and barefoot, wearing only a pair of grey sweats. He knows seeing him in sweats is a weakness for me and he isn't above exploiting said weakness.

"Years ago, a little girl with crooked pigtails stood on my front porch all shy and buck toothed. I thought she would be annoying like my sister." I glare at his description of me as a child. He slowly makes his way toward me as he speaks, "As time went on and the girl was around more, I found she wasn't annoying, she interested me and had me hanging on to every word she said. I had no idea until the girl ran when she was fifteen that I was madly and deeply in love with her." Tears burn my eyes as he stops in front of me, grabs both my hands and holds them in his as he looks down at me. "When I finally found the girl with my half-brother, I wanted to storm through the door of his house and throw her over my shoulder and bring her home with me, where she belonged." Tears fall from my eyes. He reaches up and swipes them away with his thumbs. "I didn't. I knew if I did that, I would take away her chance at a normal life. I swore I would give her until graduation until I claimed her as my own. Fate had other ideas. When I finally saw her face to face after all those years, I was done for." A watery chuckle escapes me and he smiles shyly at me. "From the moment you woke up in that dorm room, I knew I would do anything, kill anyone to have you with me always, Kiara. You are everything to me. I've never wanted something for myself before but fuck, I want you. No, I need you."

"You have me, Bishop." A whoosh of air escapes him as he slowly lowers himself to one knee in front of me. I gasp, tears fall down my cheeks as I stare down at the man I love with every fiber of my being. He releases my right hand as he digs into his pocket and pulls out a black velvet box. I reach up and cover my mouth with my hand. He flicks the lid open and sitting there nestled in its cushion is the biggest ring I have ever seen. Diamonds wrap around the outside of a perfect pale blue diamond that matches the color of my eyes.

"I said you didn't have a choice before. I know a good man would say he was wrong and give you a choice but I've never claimed to be a good man, baby. I want you forever, I want to live life with you. I want kids with you. Make me the happiest fucking man in the world, Kiara, and say yes. If you don't, I'll fuck you into submission until you scream yes!" I grip his face between my hands and smash my lips against his, my tears fall on his face but I don't care. For the first time in my life, I get the happy ending, I live by a quote every day, *start before you're ready, don't prepare, just begin.*

Bishop pulls back and looks up at me. "So, is that a yes or am I fucking a yes out of you?" I laugh as I nod my head.

"Yes, to both." He grabs the ring out of its box and slips it on my finger. I stare at the huge rock that weighs my finger down and smile. He grips my face and kisses me until I'm breathless, this kiss consumes me to the point I don't know where he begins and I end. He releases my face and doesn't break our kiss as he grips the front of my towel and yanks it open, only then does he pull back. The heated look in his eyes sends a shiver down my spine. Anticipation thrums through me when he grips the waistband of his pants and pushes them down. His cock springs free and slaps against his navel. My mouth waters at the sight, wanting to taste him on my tongue. I dart my tongue out to moisten my lips. As his eyes track my movement, he grips his cock in his hand and pumps it twice only stopping when a hiss escapes him. I clench my thighs together trying to alleviate the ache he has caused between them.

"Get on the bed, head down, ass up." I do as he says and crawl on to the bed, feeling the petals crush beneath my weight. I shiver as he runs his hands from the back of my neck down to my ass, grips my cheeks in his hands and squeezes. I moan. He lifts his left hand and lands a swift smack to my ass causing me to cry out. "I'm going to fuck this tight asshole real soon, baby." I feel myself grow wet at the thought of having him ramming his cock in my asshole. He spreads my cheeks and blows on my hole. I shift forward in surprise and earn myself another smack that has me jumping. "Stay still or I'll keep making this ass red." I've never been good at following instructions, I push back toward him and this time, he slaps both my cheeks making me cry out in pleasure. "Is my pussy dripping for me?"

"Yes." I can hear how breathless and needy I sound but

I don't give a fuck, Bishop has taken me every night, multiple times since when we came back here. We still stay in the pool house because I hate being inside that house, but also because he says I scream too loud when he fucks me. He isn't wrong. He fucked me in his office the other day and everyone in the house heard.

"You dirty girl, I can see how fucking wet you are." He kneels behind me and spreads my pussy open with his fingers, swipes his tongue up my slit making me cry out in pleasure. He licks my asshole and when he pushes his tongue inside my ass I begin to tremble with pleasure. "Fuck, you taste so good, baby. I love your cunt." I don't respond as all thought flees me when he pushes his tongue inside my pussy and pinches my clit between his fingers. I push back against his face and grind on it. He pulls back and stands leaving me panting and needy for him. "I'm going to fucking wreck this pussy so fucking bad. You gonna be a good girl and take it hard, aren't you?"

"Fuck yes."

"That's my dirty girl." I feel him line his cock up with my opening. He doesn't ease inside me, he slams in until he is balls deep making me scream. He grips my hips in a punishing grip as he fucks me like a man possessed. I grip the sheets trying to hold on, the force of his thrusts continues to push me up the bed. He slows his pace and releases my hips as he yanks me back by my hair, then grips the front of my throat and pulls me until I'm flush against his chest. I turn to the side and capture his lips in a heated kiss as he fucks me. I moan into his mouth when his cock hits that sweet spot inside me. He breaks the kiss and looks me in the eyes. "You're going to come all over my cock, baby?"

"God, yes. I'm so fucking close. Make me come and

destroy my cunt, baby." A devilish smile spreads across his face as he continues to slam inside me, over and over again until I scream his name. He releases his hold on me and pulls out. I spin around and slip off the bed knowing exactly what he wants. I drop to my knees in front of him and lock my arms behind my back and open my mouth. He grips the back of my head and holds me in place as he slams in my mouth making me gag around his cock, he's too big for me to take all the way but it never stops him from trying.

"Your pussy was too fucking good. I'm not gonna last, so fucking suck me good like I know you can!" I do as he commands and bob on his cock whilst licking him at the same time. I hollow my cheeks making sure I give him the best fucking BJ of his life. His thrusts become erratic and his grip on me tightens, he's about to come. He yanks his glorious cock from my mouth and holds my head steady as he pumps himself twice before roaring my name and shooting jets of his cum all over my face. I keep my mouth open the whole time and when a string of cum lands on my tongue I swallow and moan at the taste of him. His breaths are coming in fast pants, then he releases my hair and smears his cum all over my face making sure to rub it in. "You've never looked more beautiful. I love seeing my cum all over your face." My cunt clenches and I already want him inside me again. "Get on the fucking bed and open your legs, I want to eat your cunt until you come all over my face, then I'm going to fuck you so hard you won't be able to walk tomorrow."

Fuck I love him.

Epilogue

Bishop

6 weeks later...

The gun shot on my shoulder burns but I ignore it as we exit the restaurant that holds the bodies of the leader of the Ramano family and his underboss. I look around the parking lot and when I don't see King's car, I grind my teeth. I look to my left and flick my head for Mav to follow me, I don't stop until I reach my Tesla.

"You good, boss?" I grunt my answer, I know Kiara is going to be pissed when I get home and she finds out I've been shot again. A thrill runs through me at the thought, whenever I piss her off, she takes it out on my cock and fuck me, it's the best type of punishment I have ever had in my life. The girl likes to fuck every spare second we have together. She blew me under the blanket in the cinema room while Rook sat opposite us last weekend. I'm sure the sly fuck knew what we were up to but said nothing.

"Where the fuck is King?" Mav looks nervous and Mav never fucking gets nervous not even when he is faced with a dozen armed men. "Where the fuck is he?"

"Are you asking me as the Don or as King's brother?" I speak through clenched teeth as I answer him.

"I just got shot because he wasn't here to watch my six, I'm fucking telling you as the boss to answer me!" He nods his head and steals his shoulders.

"He knows about what you did to Christine."

Fuck!

I slouch against my car. "How did he find out?"

"That, I don't know."

"How much does he know? Does he know about Knight?" Mav shakes his head.

"I don't think so, I think he just knows about her and that's it." I nod and jump in my car to leave him and Luka behind to clean up the mess and get my men sorted, as of tonight my army just grew. We gave the Ramano soldier's a choice, die or pledge to serve me in the coming war against the Russian's, they chose to live.

I slam the front door open and storm through the house, I round the corner of the lounge and find King in the kitchen with Rook and Kiara. Kiara jumps to her feet when she sees the blood on my shirt. I ignore her and head straight for my brother. Rook grips her arm holding her back as I wrap my hand around King's throat and slam him back against the fridge, getting right in his face.

"Where the fuck were you?" He doesn't cower, he stands tall and holds my gaze.

"Visiting the grave of the woman you killed!" I ignore the gasps from behind me and keep my face blank.

"You fucking left me to deal with this shit. You were supposed to watch my back."

"You killed the fucking woman I loved, you son of a bitch!"

"You don't know shit, King!" He shoves me back and I allow it, a foot of space separates us as we glare at the other.

"What don't I know, Bishop? What else are you fucking hiding?" Bitterness coats each of his words.

"The truth, you don't know the truth!" King closes the space between us and lands a right hook. I hit back and we trade a few blows before Rook pushes him back and Kiara jumps in front of me. My nose is bleeding but not broken. His cheek is split and a slow trickle of blood seeps out.

"When the fuck were you going to tell me I had a fucking kid?" he shouts. My eyes widen and all the fight drains from my body. Kiara stares up at me in shock. I shake my head telling her I had no fucking idea about a kid. "When were you going to tell me, you killed the mother to my fucking child, Bishop?"

THANK YOU!

Thank you, Thank you, Thank you for reading my book!

I can not tell you how much this book means to me!

I never thought I would make the leap to try contemporary but I am so fucking glad I did.

The Murdoch boys are the best and thanks to Bishop never getting out of my head. I finally wrote his book. He and Kiara will always hold a place in my heart. They gave me the courage to make the leap in genres.

A massive thank you for reading their book, I do hope you loved them as much as I do!

Please if you loved the book leave a review on **Amazon, Bookbub** or **Goodreads**, it would mean a lot to hear your feedback.

The next book in the series is **Tormented By The King**

Blurb

King

She's committed a crime against the family, against me, one that no one would ever get away with.

How is it possible then that, I want to strangle the life out of her and at the same time breath life back into her lungs?

I'm the underboss, it's my job to make her pay for her crimes.

And make her pay I will.....

Allison

My sister warned me that he'll come looking. Warned me to keep Amelia away from him.

I won't let a monster like that near my niece, I don't care if she rightfully belongs to him or not.

I will protect her at any cost, even if it cost me my own heart.

Checkmate King, this Queen will overturn you.

ALSO BY SAMANTHA BARRETT

The Dream Series

The Dream Trilogy

A Beautiful Dream

A Twisted Fate

A Beautiful Nightmare

Redemption

Anarchy

Brutal Savages

Savage Lies

Brutal Truth

Savage Beast

Brutal Beauty

Murdoch Mafia Series

Played By The Bishop

Tormented By The King

Tortured By The Knight

Tempted By The Queen

Turned By The Pawn

ACKNOWLEDGMENTS

My baby daddy, my husband, thank you. No long novel needed, you know I love you like a hussy loves dick.

Elizabeth, thank you for editing Bishop and polishing him up to make him as perfect as he is.

Tash, what to say? Thank you doesn't seem enough. You helped me more than you will ever know and stood by me while I raged and cried about this book. You are the best!

My Beta team! Fuck, you girls are so beyond amazing. Thank you all for loving Bish and pushing me to keep going.

My street and ARC team. I love you all dearly. From the bottom of my heart, thank you!

My readers.
I love you. Thank you for trusting me to deliver the best story and following me. Without you none of this would be possible.

Xxxx
Sam

ABOUT THE AUTHOR

Samantha is a book lover and writer. She is originally from the land of the long white cloud, New Zealand.
She can also talk the ears off a donkey!
Samantha loves anything Twilight and is a TWIHARD proudly.

She loves fantasy-romance novels with strong Alpha males. Samantha loves to write complicated love stories with a twist. A strong heroine is a must!

She lives in Brisbane, Australia with her husband, two children, and three dogs.

If her books leave you wanting more or you feel as if you connected with the characters in some way, she takes that as a win!!
Samantha loves writing anything that is out of the box!

www.ingramcontent.com/pod-product-compliance
Lightning Source LLC
Chambersburg PA
CBHW020519120726
47904CB00003B/892